The Original Freddie Ackerman

Also by Hadley Irwin

O

ABBY, MY LOVE
BRING TO A BOIL AND SEPARATE
CAN'T HEAR YOU LISTENING
I BE SOMEBODY
KIM / KIMI
MOON AND ME
SO LONG AT THE FAIR
WHAT ABOUT GRANDMA?

(Margaret K. McElderry Books)

O

THE LILITH SUMMER
WE ARE MESQUAKIE, WE ARE ONE

O

WRITING YOUNG ADULT NOVELS
(with Jeannette Eyerly)

The Original Freddie Ackerman

HADLEY IRWIN

Margaret K. McElderry Books   New York

Maxwell Macmillan Canada • Toronto

Maxwell Macmillan International

New York • Oxford • Singapore • Sydney

Margaret K. McElderry Books
Macmillan Publishing Company
866 Third Avenue, New York, NY 10022

Maxwell Macmillan Canada, Inc.
1200 Eglinton Avenue East, Suite 200
Don Mills, Ontario M3C 3N1

Macmillan Publishing Company is part of the
Maxwell Communication Group of Companies.

First edition
Printed in the United States of America
10 9 8 7 6 5 4 3 2 1

Library of Congress Cataloging-in-Publication Data
Irwin, Hadley. The original Freddie Ackerman / Hadley
Irwin. — 1st ed.   p.   cm.
Summary: Twelve-year-old Trevor Frederick Ackerman refuses
to spend another summer with his extended family of divorced
parents, stepparents, and stepbrothers and stepsisters, so he is
sent up to Maine to stay with two eccentric great-aunts and there
gets involved with some interesting people and an unexpected
mystery.
ISBN 0-689-50562-0
[1. Great-aunts—Fiction.   2. Islands—Fiction.
3. Maine—Fiction.]   I. Title.   PZ7.I712Or
1992 [Fic]—dc20   91-43145

For MARTY and GRACE
of Skyefield

The Original Freddie Ackerman

ALL THE OTHER PASSENGERS on his flight had been met, hugged, kissed, and hurried off to waiting cars while Trevor Frederick Ackerman sat alone in the midst of his luggage.

Two flight attendants hurried by, pulling suitcases on tiny wheels. One of them glanced at him, grinned, and called, "Good-bye, Freddie Ackerman. Don't forget to write." He watched them disappear down the concourse, where a new line of travelers was forming in front of the ticket counter. The woman in the Avis Rental Car booth kept glancing over at him as if she thought he was either a runaway or an abandoned child.

That was the problem with being twelve. Even when he was dressed in Lands' End moccasins, slacks, shirt, and sweater, people still saw only the twelve-year-old Trevor. It wasn't easy looking twelve and having to act twenty-one. When he was eleven, his halves matched. No matter how he turned the numbers, they still came out eleven; but that was before his meaningful relationship with Jessica.

"Someone forget you?" a maintenance man asked as he stopped to empty a rubbish container beside Trevor.

"No," Trevor answered as if he believed what he was saying.

What if they *had* forgotten him? What if no one *did* come to get him? At least then he wouldn't have to face the weeks ahead. What if he disappeared? What if he became Freddie Ackerman full time? Freddie Ackerman wouldn't be waiting in a strange airport for someone he'd never seen. Freddie Ackerman would call for a skycap and find a taxi.

Trevor Frederick Ackerman continued to sit and wait, hoping someone would remember him. Not that he wasn't acquainted with airports. He practically had his own personal jet stream out to Real-Father and Other-Mother-Daphne and back to Real-Mom and Other-Father-Norman, only now it was New-Other-Father-Charlie, but he'd forget about that.

He dug through his backpack and pulled out his Walkman. Adjusting the earphones, he turned up the volume and hoped the beat of the Grateful Dead, with their reverbs and zydecos, would drown out thoughts he didn't want to think.

2

Mom and New-Other-Father-Charlie would probably be in Bermuda by now, though a honeymoon was a little silly since Charlie had been practically living with them for the past six months. When Mom had told him about Charlie's photographic assignment in Bermuda and how the two of them intended to combine that with "time together," all Trevor could say was, "What about me?"

That became the big question. It was too late to register him for summer camp, and he absolutely refused to spend that much time with Real-Father and Other-Mother-Daphne and their three *thems* and two little *its*, Roy and Ray, who couldn't pronounce *r*'s, so they called themselves Woy and Way. Everybody thought it was cute. Trevor didn't.

That left the great-aunts, whom Mom had dredged up from a place called Blue Isle in Maine.

He headed for the candy machine. Maybe some M&M's would help his stomach. He wasn't homesick. There wasn't anyone at home, so how could he be homesick for an empty second-floor apartment? Anyway, sometimes he got homesick at home when everyone was gone. Of course there was Jessica, but he wasn't going to think about her anymore after what she had done.

The M&M's tasted funny. Jessica said green ones tasted better than brown, so she always grabbed them first, but since she was no longer his significant other, he picked out all the greens for himself, even though they didn't taste any better.

"Are you Trevor Ackerman?"

He yanked off his earphones and hung them around his neck.

The tiny, white-haired woman wore a strange cap, a leather beret-thing with a sagging bill that almost hid her faded blue eyes.

She needn't have asked. There was no one else around but him.

"I'm to pick you up. Your Aunt Calla doesn't do airports. I'm your Aunt Louisa."

"Great-Aunt Louisa?" He tried not to stare. Her face was tanned and lined, but even standing still, she looked as if she were in motion.

"Whatever." She looked down at his luggage, picked up his two bags, and started for the exit. Trevor threw his backpack over his shoulder and hurried to catch up with her. It was raining outside the terminal, turning the entire world an ugly gray.

"Wait here. I'll bring the car around," she ordered, setting the bags down, hunching her shoulders, and disappearing into the rain.

"They're family," his mother had explained. "They're your grandaunts, really, your grandmother's younger sisters. Louisa after Louisa May Alcott and Calla after some flower, I think."

Great-Aunt Louisa didn't look sturdy enough to be a regular aunt, let alone a great-aunt.

A big maroon station wagon with sides paneled in real wood finally pulled up to the curb. His great-aunt hopped out and stacked his luggage in the back while he crawled into the front seat. Automatically, he reached for the seat belt. There wasn't one! The wagon was so old that it must have been made before he was born!

"It's about an hour's drive," she said as they pulled out of the airport. She sounded younger than she looked. She wasn't much taller than he—frail-looking, really— but he'd heard once that when people got old they began to shrink.

"What's it like on Blue Isle?"

"Quiet." Her eyes never left the road. Then, when he thought she wasn't going to say anything more, she went on. "Blue Isle is lovely. Trees, sky, ocean. Enchanting, really."

Sure. The Land of Oz, and she was Glinda the Good Witch. Trevor almost said it aloud, but he'd learned to keep Freddie Ackerman remarks to himself.

"What's there to do?"

"Whatever you like."

"I mean, are there malls? Movies? Video-game arcades?"

"No."

The word sounded as final as a death sentence. He had thought he was escaping from the *its* and *thems*. This was no escape. This was exile!

They crossed a nameless river. He knew they were headed south because he'd looked at a map, but now in the rain he couldn't read any of the road signs. At one place, on the far edge of the city, road construction blocked one lane. As they waited for the traffic light to turn green, he wondered what would happen if he opened the car door and disappeared. Great-Aunt Calla would probably be relieved, and Great-Aunt Louisa, sitting beside him, might not even notice, since she hadn't looked over at him yet and, besides that, seemed to have used up her quota of words for the day.

Freddie Ackerman, World War II ace, his B-24 Liberator bomber shot down in flames and his parachute buried deep in the Black Forest, would never allow himself to be captured alive with all the secret invasion plans he was carrying. Freddie Ackerman would fling open the car door, slide down into the river that bordered the autobahn, and fade like a ghost into the rain and mist of the German countryside.

He'd seen every World War II movie that the video store owned. Jessica said it was very important to learn about World War II, but that was before she got hooked on space shuttles.

The windshield wipers on the old station wagon beat like wings against the downpour of rain. The highway finally narrowed down to two lanes as the houses began to thin out, so there was nothing to see but gray highway, gray sky, gray rain.

Jessica told him once that whenever she felt terribly alone and sad, she thought about beautiful colors like aqua blue or sunset orange or dusty rose. She said he had to say the actual words as well as think the colors, or it wouldn't work. Trevor tried thinking of beautiful colors:

banana yellow, celery green, beet red, but no matter how hard he tried, all he got was hungry. When he remembered what Jessica had said that last week of school, his colors faded.

The road began to turn and twist with sudden hills, not high, and valleys, not deep, but always trees on either side, blotting out the rest of the world.

"We understand your mother is remarrying."

It wasn't something he wanted to talk about, but at least the Silent One knew he was sitting there.

"It's already happened. They're in Bermuda by now. When they said, 'I do,' I wished they didn't." He stared at the dashboard. It was so clean and shiny it looked as if it belonged in a brand-new car. "So now I have *three* fathers. I've had *two* mothers practically forever."

They slowed down to wait their turn to pass a truck and she looked over at him as if she were going to say something important, but all that came out was "Oh?"

He didn't tell her about the *its* or the *thems*. It was too complicated. He had a whole family of *thems*—three stepbrothers (besides the *its*) from Other-Mother-Daphne, two new stepsisters who were coming with New-Other-Father-Charlie, and a stepbrother and a stepsister from Other-Father-Norman. Of course, New-Other-Father-Charlie's first wife had married someone else too, and they had two kids. He wasn't sure what relation they would be. Once-removed-stepbrother and once-removed-stepsister, maybe. That would make Charlie's first wife Trevor's ex-once-removed-stepmother and Other-Mother-

Daphne's first husband his ex-once-removed-stepfather. It almost made him carsick. Back in fifth grade, he had had to draw his family tree. It looked like a jungle, and there wasn't any room for him.

"She thought it would be good for me. Coming here. Sharpen my coping skills."

"Your mother?"

"My shrink."

"Your shrink!"

"My therapist." If she didn't understand *shrink*, her brain was on hold.

"Something wrong with you?"

She was no different. Grown-ups never talked. They only asked questions.

"That's the problem. They think I'm too controlled . . . that I should act out. She said I had too many authority figures in my life. I think she meant parents."

"You mean you're mixed up?" She turned and really looked at him, then hurried to look back at the road.

"My family is. Anyway, my shrink told me I was supposed to discard all my role models so that I can discover who I am. Do you know who you are?"

She smiled, then bit one corner of her mouth. "I'm too old for all that. I worry about who I've been."

"This summer I'm supposed to experience behavior modification and self-actualization. Charlie, my new father, says it means doing my own thing. I don't know what my own thing is. Do you?"

"At my age, does it matter?"

Between sweeps of the windshield wipers, he could see an occasional house, firewood stacked by the front porch, and sometimes signs advertising craft shops, wood carvings, pottery, and original oil paintings. He wished he were back home in his own bedroom. Once he'd sneaked out, when everyone thought he was asleep, and met Jessica, and they'd gone to an all-night video arcade. It didn't make much sense now, but at the time it had been fun. It wasn't the end of the world without Jessica, but it was close.

He watched the odometer as it slowly rolled off the tenths of miles and, eventually, the miles. He closed his eyes to see if he could guess the exact second when the mile number rolled into its little slot. He missed it by two-tenths the first time, but after nine or ten tries, he hit it right at the exact moment.

When he used to ride along with Mom and Charlie, he'd sit in the backseat of Charlie's Audi and make up songs that he sang to himself, inside his head, songs that didn't mean anything—just songs without words, the kind all people sing to themselves when they're feeling alone.

A sleek white convertible honked loudly and sped by them as the station wagon, grinding away in second gear, crawled up a long hill.

"Some people drive as though they have to get there yesterday," his great-aunt grumbled. "From here on, however, the hills aren't so steep. Only trouble is the valleys are deeper."

Trevor wasn't sure whether she was trying to make a joke or if she really believed what she was saying. "That couldn't be, could it?" He had learned it was smart to act dumb around adults, particularly when they were attempting to be funny.

"Of course not!" The corner of her mouth moved as if she were going to smile, but decided not to.

The sky suddenly grew lighter and, at the top of a hill, trees thinned and, below, water in a bay spread like a gray sheet with a string of hills beyond. Then came a high bridge.

"The causeway, and then it's Blue Isle." She sounded like a tour director. All Trevor could see was mud.

"Clammers out there. See them? Raking for clams while the tide's out."

A big black Lab bounded around barking at the retreating tide, and then ahead was the island, looking as if it had been shoved out to sea in the hope that it would float away.

Great-Aunt Louisa might think Blue Isle was enchanting, but Trevor couldn't see any signs of its magic. Once they were across the causeway, the road curled and twisted up and down, over hills and through solid walls of fir trees as uniform as matchsticks.

"Mom says," he began, after neither of them had spoken for at least five minutes, "that Great-Aunt Calla sells books. Is her store along here someplace?"

"She doesn't have a store. And sometimes I think she keeps more than she sells. But we're almost there," she added, slowing down even more and making a sharp right turn.

The problem was where *there* was. They were on a one-lane drive, moving through a green tunnel of trees while his great-aunt hunched over the wheel, steering, Trevor was sure, by the ornament on the hood of the car. Finally, the drive bent suddenly, trees parted, and there was a lawn outlined by a split-rail fence.

"And here's Skyfield," she announced, stopping the station wagon with a sudden jerk.

The house, two-storied, blue-shuttered, with weathered clapboards, was huge, not so much high as wide and long. His aunt gathered up his luggage and started toward the rear of the house. Trevor disentangled himself from his Walkman, picked up his backpack, and followed. She opened a door and nodded him through. The door wasn't even locked. It was hard to imagine a door without bolts and chains and bells and alarms, but after all, this *was* an island, not civilization.

They walked through an anteroom with a brick floor and a drain in the middle. A bunch of rubber boots were clumped in one corner, with sweaters and jackets and slickers hung unevenly on hooks above them. At the end of the room, an old wooden table sagged under the weight of a huge stack of magazines and books and several sick-looking houseplants. In another corner, a spindly potted tree leaned drunkenly against the wall.

"Mudroom," his aunt explained and motioned Trevor ahead.

11

He was finally inside, standing in a hallway that ran the full depth of the house from front to back. The wide boards under his feet were smooth, as if they had been polished by generations of people. Far down the hall he could see the blue flicker of logs burning in a fireplace, and from somewhere came soft music.

"It's your aunt Calla's private time. I'll show you where your room is." She looked up at the grandfather clock that loomed against the wall. "Why don't you unpack, wash up a bit, and come down in . . . say twenty minutes." It was not a question.

Trevor followed her again, this time up the stairs, an open stairway with broad steps and a wide banister, then down a hall and into a bedroom.

"My sister is a precise person. She'll see you in twenty minutes." She paused at the door as if she'd forgotten something, then asked, "Do you have any bad habits we should know about?"

"I don't think so."

"You won't mind being by yourself for a while, will you?"

"No." Then he added, in his best twenty-one-year-old Trevor Frederick Ackerman voice, "I'm an expert at being alone."

"Really?" She backed out into the hall, her hand still on the doorknob. "I guess I'm not young enough to be an expert at that," and she closed the door gently.

This was Weirdsville! Had his mother realized what

the place was like? He turned and looked around the room. It was very big—bigger than both his and his mom's bedrooms at home put together—with wide floorboards like the ones downstairs, partly covered with a blue-and-white rug. Across the room two large windows, with a broad window seat beneath jutted out toward the bay. There was also an honest-to-goodness four-poster bed, a big dresser, something he thought was probably used as a closet, and a rolltop desk like the kind he used to see in antique shops the summer his mom was on her Early American kick.

He walked toward another door, hoping it didn't open into someone else's room. It didn't. He had his *own* bathroom! It was almost half the size of the bedroom, and the toilet had some kind of tank high above it on the wall, and the bathtub with its claw feet looked big enough to swim in. A private bathroom! He couldn't believe it. It had been bad enough when Mom and he shared a bathroom, but when Charlie moved in with his razor and his bathrobe and stuff, there was no privacy at all.

He sat on the edge of the bed. Should he change his clothes? Just his shirt and sweater, maybe. Something made him dig down into his bag and pull out the T-shirt Mom didn't know he'd packed. He and Jessica had each bought one down at the Dare-You-Wear T-shirt store at the mall. It had Intelligence Is the Ultimate Aphrodisiac printed in red across the front. He'd unpack the rest later, but now for Great-Aunt Calla.

The stairway swept down, the banister a shining expanse of polished walnut ending in a graceful swirl at the bottom. He'd seen stairways like it on TV, but he'd never actually been in a house big enough to have one. He rubbed one hand across the glossy surface and looked down to the hall beneath. He was used to hearing, "When in doubt, Trevor, don't!" He usually didn't, but Freddie Ackerman knew that if he did something he really wanted to do and acted as if he didn't know it was wrong, he could do almost anything and get away with it.

There was no sound from the rooms below. Trevor hesitated. Freddie Ackerman didn't. With one leap, Freddie Ackerman was straddling the banister and sailing down so fast he didn't have time to ready himself for a landing. He zoomed off the end of the banister like a bullet and landed on his hands and knees, hitting the bare floor with a thump that echoed down the hall. For a few seconds he didn't move. When he didn't hear anything, he got up, pulled down his T-shirt, and waited for his Great-Aunt Calla to appear in the first stages of panic.

She didn't.

Trevor walked over to the heavy French doors and peered through. A fire burned in the fireplace and a large woman, her back toward him, stood resting one arm up against the mantel as she stared down into the fire.

"Rough landing?" She didn't turn around.

Trevor took a deep breath. "Relatively."

"You mean yes, I presume?" She turned to look at

him, her eyes an icy blue. She wasn't just large! She was *huge*! And her voice was bigger yet.

"Yes." She was watching him, and it made him itch in places he couldn't reach. "I mean yes, I meant yes." She wore a funny robelike dress that looked as if it might have come from Africa, large gold hoop earrings, a necklace made of seashells, and everything else about her *was* her—lots of *her*! Jessica would have said she was drenched in calories.

He tried to look out the window, but he could feel her eyes measuring him from the prickles at the base of his neck down to his heels, where his new moccasins had worn a blister. The rain had stopped, and beyond the lawn, water gleamed a steely silver below a ridge of far hills.

"What's over there?" he asked. "Another island?" Ask questions when you can't think of anything else to say, Jessica always told him.

He wasn't interested in a geography lesson, but at least his great-aunt quit looking at him and gazed out the window, too.

"Camden Hills. They're over on the mainland. 'The mountains look on Marathon. And Marathon looks on the sea,' " she recited. "That's Lord Byron. The water is Penobscot Bay. We're on a little cove of that bay here at Skyfield."

He was getting the geography lesson, anyway, plus Lord Byron, whoever he was.

"How far is it across? To the mainland, I mean."

"Too far to swim. A bit tricky to sail. Altogether, it's a world away." She gestured toward the window seat. "Won't you sit down? If we're going to spend the summer together, we really should become acquainted. We have nearly an hour before dinner."

An hour! An entire sixty-minute hour? It might as well be a lifetime! Not that he was hungry, but what could they possibly talk about for that long?

There was no need to worry. This great-aunt had a full hour of questions saved up for him. She eased herself down into a plush easy chair, propped her feet up on a matching ottoman, and asked, "And how is your mother?"

"Which one?" Trevor glanced out the window again, wondering how long it would take to row a boat across to the mainland. When he looked back at his aunt, she was coughing a polite little cough and staring at something just above his head.

"Your own mother, Trevor. Millicent."

"Oh, she's fine. At least she was this morning when they left. They should be in Bermuda by now." He tried to sound as if it didn't make any difference to him where they were or how they were.

"Well, I sincerely hope your mother has made the right choice this time."

"I hope so, too. She should know by the end of the summer. I don't believe in that happily-ever-after stuff, do you?"

His aunt didn't answer right away. Instead she searched through the pocket of her dress and, slipping a little white lozenge into her mouth, said, "His name is Charlie, isn't it?"

"Yes," he answered, wondering when she was going to start fixing dinner. "Norman was the one before Charlie. Dad was before Norman."

"Oh yes, I remember." She was gazing past him again. "And what about your own father? You see him regularly, I suppose. He remarried, too, didn't he?"

She was answering her own questions. Maybe that way she could be sure of getting the answers she wanted. Or maybe it was easier to think up questions if you already knew the answers. "Yes," he finally said. He tried not to sound bored. She didn't ask about the *its* and the *thems*, and he was glad.

He knew they were through with the family when she asked, "And how is school? Fine, no doubt."

She was like all the rest of them. Whenever there was nothing else to talk to kids about, they always asked the same stupid question: How's school? School was school. Boring! Boring! Boring!

"A rose is a rose is a rose," he muttered, looking around the room. There were so many pictures, it was like an art gallery.

"That's a Gertrude Stein line! How on earth do you know that?" She sounded as shocked as though he'd said a four-letter word.

"Heard it on a game show. You know. TV. 'Jeopardy!' or one of those." He didn't think she understood, so he added, "School's fine, I guess."

"What do you like best about it?"

"June, July, August." He thought maybe she'd laugh a little, but instead she merely raised an eyebrow. "I mean," he went on, not too sure where he was going, "school's all right. They have to do something with us until we're old enough to go to work."

His great-aunt rubbed her forehead. Her hands matched the rest of her—smooth and soft and white. They had run out of things to say. Where was the other aunt? The little one? This one, silhouetted against the glare of the late-afternoon sun streaming in through the side window, was a faceless shadow, like those people on TV who appear like black blobs so that no one can recognize them.

Trevor turned away and looked out the opposite window. He wished he were a long-distance swimmer and could run down across the lawn, plunge into the bay, and strike out for the mainland—only he hadn't even passed out of Polliwogs last summer at camp.

He wished he'd changed into his jeans. His slacks were too loose where they should have been tight, his Jockey shorts were twisted off center, and every time he moved, the woman kept staring at the printing on his T-shirt. Finally, he could stand the silence no longer. "Are they paying you for keeping me?"

"Paying us?" She stood up and walked over toward the fireplace. "Of course not! Your mother wrote and asked if you could come and stay, and we said yes, if *you* wanted to. After all, you're family." She stopped, cleared her throat, and went on. "But what made you decide to come here rather than go to your own father's?"

Trevor looked down at his moccasins. "To tell the truth," he began in his best Trevor Frederick Ackerman voice, "I was tired of feeling like some sort of bone disease. The judge called it joint custody."

He could see at once that his great-aunt did not think that remark very funny, either. He did. It wasn't original, though. Jessica had told him that was what he suffered from.

"Actually," he began again, "I kind of needed time off or time out or whatever." Then suddenly he was pretty sure he knew the answer that would stop all her questions. "You see . . . when I'm out with . . . my real dad and Daphne . . . I'm . . . well . . . you know . . . like we're supposed to be a blended family and all that . . . but what I do mostly out there is baby-sit and. . . ." He let his words trail off in a suggestion of a sigh. Jessica had told him once that that was most effective on parents. Jessica read a lot of romance novels.

It must have worked because his great-aunt nodded. "I see your point."

He waited for her to go on, but she didn't. He knew it was his turn to say something, but his mind went blank. Jessica had a theory that when a person was caught without a single idea, all he had to do was put his right index finger over his right nostril and breathe through the left side of his nose. Jessica swore that was how she got through exams without studying. It was worth a try. He put his finger beside his nose and waited for the thoughts. Maybe it would have been easier to tell his great-aunt the truth: "Mom dumped me here because she and Charlie didn't want me around, and no one else did either."

"Is something wrong?" She leaned toward him. "Do you need a Kleenex?"

"No." He took his hand from his nose. "I was just thinking. Do you ever have trouble believing what you're thinking?" He was being honest.

"I'm not sure I understand what you're trying to say." She didn't sound impatient, exactly. She sounded more as if she were trying to translate something from a foreign language, but the way she looked over at him made Trevor want to explain.

"It's like dreaming. You know it's a dream, of course, but you wonder where it comes from, and sometimes that's the way thinking works, too." Jessica's finger-on-the-nose trick really worked! He tried again to explain because his great-aunt was looking at him as if she were really seeing him this time. "Twelve is a particularly difficult age, don't you think?"

She looked around the room as if she didn't know where she was. "I'm not sure I know what it's like to be twelve, though I must have been once. I can't remember whether I knew too much at twelve or too little. Maybe at twelve we know everything we need to know to survive. But enough now. We'll have more time to find out this summer, won't we? Now . . ." She started toward the hall. "What do you need to know, I wonder, about Skyfield?"

"Rules, I suppose." Other-Mother-Daphne's rules, neatly typed, were posted on the refrigerator door for him, all beginning with *don't*.

"Your time on Blue Isle is your own. I'm sure you can manage that. There are plenty of books to read in the library. Your room is yours to do with as you wish, of course. Your mother says you're quite self-sufficient, so you can get your own breakfast. You'll find the refrigerator well stocked."

He could hear his mom: "He'll be no bother." That's what she always said.

"And as for rules . . . 'Where no law is, there is no transgression.' That's from the Bible, you know. King James version." She paused, studying him as if she were attempting to guess his weight. "Let's forget rules. Let's have an understanding instead. I work in the morning. After lunch I nap and read. Then I have tea, which is my private time. Dinner's at seven."

She sounded tired.

"And now I have a few things to attend to. Why don't you explore the house. We'll call you when it's time to eat."

Skyfield wasn't like any other home he'd ever been

in. In apartments, he could tell right away where every room was. This place was full of surprises. He'd think he was walking into a kitchen, only it would be a den, and what he supposed was another bedroom turned out to be the library, filled with books stacked on shelves that ran from floor to ceiling on all sides. He sat down in a big leather chair by a window that looked out over an expanse of trees. What a downer! Mom might as well have dropped him off at the public library for the summer.

He hadn't seen a single TV set—anywhere! Not in the fireplace room. Not in the big living room. Not even in the library. How could his mother do this to him? He'd never find out who the killer was on "Mystery!" He'd miss "Nova" and "Jeopardy!" and "Night Court." All they had here were books. He could feel them crowding in on him from all sides. If Great-Aunt Calla sold books, why didn't she get rid of some of these and make a fortune?

A faint tinkle of a distant bell, followed by, "Trevor, it's time for dinner," and Great Aunt Calla appeared and guided him down the hall to a side door he'd not seen. Suddenly they were in a completely different house. A table was set for three, and in the small kitchenette stood his other great-aunt, the little one. Trevor had begun to think he'd imagined her. She motioned him toward a chair, and then turned back to the stove where something was making a peculiar smell. Without thinking, Trevor crinkled his nose. Great-Aunt Calla noticed. He was sure she noticed everything. She unfolded her napkin and smiled over at him. "We're having fish tonight."

"Bouillabaisse," came the voice of Great-Aunt Louisa.

Trevor drew in a quick breath. If there was anything that made his stomach do calisthenics, it was fish.

"You'll love it, Trevor." It sounded like an order. "Louisa has her own secret recipe."

Maybe if he thought cheeseburgers, he wouldn't taste the fish. Jessica could do that. Once, on a dare, she ate a live grasshopper and pretended it was cornflakes, and she didn't even upchuck.

"On Sundays," Great-Aunt Calla went on, "we have dinner here at Louisa's. Other days, when Melva comes, we eat in the main house. At seven."

"I see. But Great-Aunt—"

"And that's another thing, Trevor." She arranged her napkin on her lap. "While we are indeed your great-aunts, we're not sure we can stand an entire summer of hearing it. Besides, it's such a waste of words."

He certainly agreed. "What should I call you?"

"What would you like to call us?"

Trevor thought for a moment. Freddie Ackerman already had several names—Calorie Cal and Lo-Cal Lou, but Trevor suggested, in his most polite voice, "Aunt Cal? That would be shorter."

"Aunt Cal," she repeated. "What do you think, Louisa? Aunt Cal?"

"Sounds good," his other aunt called from the stove.

"And I suppose I'll be Aunt Lou, only don't bother with the aunt part."

"All right, then," his great-aunt Calla said as if she were making an announcement, "Aunt Cal and Lou it will be."

"Names aren't important anyway, do you think?" Trevor looked straight into her eyes without blinking. He'd practiced doing that at home in front of the bathroom mirror when he discovered it drove Charlie crazy.

Lou set a large tureen on the table, tapped her sister gently on the shoulder and said, as if she'd won an argument, " 'Not waving but drowning.' "

Aunt Cal nodded and turned to Trevor. "Louisa is quoting from a poem. Her head works strangely sometimes, and this evening she is being poetic. She wavers between poet and saint, and now she's being a poet." Then to Lou she added, "And, being a poet, she always expects the tragic." Turning back to Trevor she said, "She hoes a narrow row, but there are no weeds in it."

Trevor had gotten lost somewhere between the drowning and the hoeing. Lou bowed an exaggerated bow and sat down at the table between Aunt Cal and Trevor. She served the stew, first a bowl to Aunt Cal and then one to Trevor.

The stew shimmered before him, with silvery lumps floating on its surface. He picked up his spoon, prodded some of the bigger globs aside and dipped up a tiny sip. He closed his eyes, trying not to think of fish, with their blank stares, slippery scales, and gaping mouths. He held his breath as the stew slipped past his tongue and slid down his throat. He felt his two aunts watching, so he hurried to dip up another spoonful.

"Perhaps you would like some bread. It's Louisa's speciality." Aunt Cal smiled across at Lou as if she were bestowing a knighthood; then she looked over at Trevor's bowl, her eyes ordering him to eat.

One good thing about the meal: There was no need for Trevor to talk. Aunt Cal and Lou did that, fragments of their conversation floating past him like the lumps of fish in his stew—long, meaningless words like *accountability*. There were several *accountability*'s plus some *paradigm*'s and *reciprocity*'s. It might as well have been some foreign language, but he was good at sitting among people and shutting out their talk and disappearing inside himself. He finished his stew by counting the spoonfuls: twenty-seven-and-a-half to empty his bowl.

"We haven't planned anything for tomorrow for you, Trevor. We could drive over to the mainland in the afternoon, if you'd like. I have a few things I have to do there someday. There is a bicycle in the small shed behind the garage," said Aunt Cal.

He watched his two aunts fold their napkins and place them beside their bowls. He folded his napkin and placed it beside his bowl. "I was going to ask you, Aunt Cal . . ."

"Yes?"

"I was wondering where your TV is. I usually watch 'Murder, She Wrote' on Sunday nights."

It was suddenly very quiet. His two aunts looked at each other.

"Well, Trevor," Lou began, not looking at him but at her sister.

"It's this way, Trevor," Aunt Cal broke in. "We don't have one. This is an island, remember?"

"No TV!" Trevor repeated, too loudly he could tell. "You must be kidding! How do you find out what's happening in the world without TV?"

"We read," Aunt Cal said, sounding like the end of an argument he didn't know had begun. "Newspapers. Magazines. Books. Louisa has a scanner, of course, for weather reports." She was watching him too closely again, and he didn't like it. "I'm sure you'll find plenty to see and read and enjoy after you've been here a few days."

"You shouldn't miss too much not having TV, hooked up permanently the way you are to that radio thing you wear. Can you sleep in it too?" Trevor did not like the way Lou smiled.

He looked down at his empty bowl. He hated Blue Isle! He hated Lou's fish stew! He hated having to spend the summer with two old ladies, and as far as he could tell, the rest of his summer was going to be as flat and boring as the water in their stupid bay! He was beginning to wonder if the second-most horrible day of his entire life would ever end. The worst was when Jessica had said . . . But Jessica was a quark!

"Now I imagine you have some unpacking left to do, and you'll want to get settled in, no doubt." Lou might as well have told him to go to his room, so taking the hint, he did—gladly.

He stretched out on his bed and stared at the ceiling. How was he going to get through a whole summer? Ninety-four days of it! He'd counted them. He could make a calendar and cross off the days, the way that man on the TV talk show did when he was imprisoned for a crime he didn't commit, but that was too depressing.

From somewhere downstairs came the quiet rise and fall of Aunt Cal's voice as she talked to Lou, and then came the music—music without words, the kind that doesn't need words to make it music.

Trevor shut his eyes and the notes appeared like patterned wallpaper of blues and reds and greens etched under his eyelids. He was Freddie Ackerman. With the slightest movement of his hands, Freddie Ackerman could become the notes and fly through the open window and sail off into the night air. He was swimming in air! Free and weightless, he skimmed over the bay and dipped above the water, brushing the tops of waves, the music following like a wisp of smoke.

When he awoke the next morning, someone had slipped off his moccasins and covered him with a blanket.

By NOON THE NEXT DAY, during his third trip through the house, Trevor had given up hoping to find anything more interesting than he'd seen the evening before. Outside, the clouds were leaking a miserable soft dripping rain; inside, the rooms were silent and empty. He didn't really want to talk to either Lou or Aunt Cal, but he wouldn't have minded hearing their voices.

He'd peered into the refrigerator, poked through the desk drawers in the library, looked at the labels on his aunts' collection of CDs, and even made a tour of the photographs that hung in the broad hallway. All of the pictures were signed, but the writing was so faded he could hardly read the names—Edna St. something, somebody named White, and someone named Franklin who was sitting in a wheelchair and holding a dog on his lap.

28

Trevor was just about to start up the stairway when Aunt Calla walked down. When she saw him, she stopped and gestured toward the kitchen.

"You've found something healthy to eat." This time she didn't even bother making it into a question. "It's all healthy, of course—terribly, terribly nutritious."

Before he could answer, she collapsed like a balloon slowly losing air and sat on the steps looking down at him, her dress billowing around her in gentle folds. She leaned toward him and whispered, "You will notice, Trevor, that it is a cholesterol-free refrigerator: skim milk; plain, fat-free yogurt, fat-free yogurt ice cream; and many, many skinless, boneless chicken breasts stacked in the freezer."

"Yes, ma'am," Trevor answered, remembering the package of Twinkies he'd discovered behind the lettuce in the veggie compartment. He'd eaten them for breakfast, along with a can of Coca-Cola Classic he'd found tucked inside a carton labeled Egg Beaters, some kind of egg substitute.

"However, since you are a growing boy who needs food that tastes like food, perhaps you could make a list of some of your favorite items. Ice-cream bars, chocolate cookies, cheese, for example?" She closed her eyes and went on. "Swiss cheese, Brie, aged cheddar. Real eggs, bacon, ham, well-marbled steak. There, doesn't that sound good?"

"And frozen pizza?" he asked.

"Brilliant, Trevor, absolutely brilliant," she said,

slowly getting to her feet. "Now, you might want to run upstairs and start your list. And if you haven't done so already, you may unpack your suitcases. The dresser is empty and you can use that for your . . . things." She sounded as if she didn't know what boys wore underneath.

He waited until she was standing in the hallway before he started up the stairs. He didn't think there was room for both of them.

She called up to him, "On rainy days like this there's not much to do but read. There are plenty of books in the library. Perhaps later we could play a game of some sort. What games do young people play these days?"

"I don't know. I'm not very fond of games, really." He thought of the poker Jessica and he used to play on rainy Saturdays when there was nothing else to do. They played for money, and sometimes he won when Jessica didn't cheat.

Aunt Cal disappeared into the kitchen, so Trevor went to his room and unpacked, stacking his underclothes neatly in the massive dresser. As long as they were in his suitcase, he hadn't felt he was marooned on Blue Isle, but more as if he were staying in some kind of bed-and-breakfast place for the night.

He sat on the edge of the bed and stared at the floor. This summer was never going to work; he knew that right down to the bottom of his Reeboks. If he wasn't floating in totally repulsive fish stew, he'd be sitting at the desk across the room making lists of fattening food. And when all of that got too exciting, he could read his way through Aunt Cal's library!

He crossed his eyes and flopped backward onto the bed. Even if they'd wanted him, which they hadn't, he would have refused to spend the summer watching Mom and Charlie play house and photograph flamingos or whatever they were taking pictures of. The *its* and *thems* made Dad and Daphne's place strictly unendurable. And Other-Father-Norman hadn't liked Trevor any better than Trevor had liked him.

As far as Skyfield and the great-aunts were concerned, he could probably fade into the sunset and they wouldn't even notice. He sat up and planted both feet on the floor. Fade into the sunset? The sun set in the west. Almost everything was west of Blue Isle, including a bay too big and wet to get across. There had to be some way to escape that didn't include Lou and her ancient station wagon.

Right now the problem wasn't so much *where* to go, but how to go *anywhere*. "Oh, go take a long bus ride, Trevor." That was one of the next-to-last things Jessica had said to him when she stopped the meaningful part of their relationship.

As soon as Trevor remembered, Freddie Ackerman was in motion, on his feet, digging out his hooded sweatshirt and racing down the stairs, through the mud-room, and out the back door. He wasn't sure how far away the village was, but he knew it existed because his aunts had been talking about it the night before.

A village meant civilization; civilization meant transportation; transportation might mean a bus that would take him off the island!

Freddie Ackerman, escaped prisoner of war, ran until his throat burned, then slowed to a fast walk. The drizzle of rain against his face was a reminder of his newly won freedom. With no weapon but his wits, he sloshed through the rain-soaked danger-filled forest. His sneakers squished out water at every step as he put captivity behind him forever.

At the crest of a hill, a small car, a Ford Escort, he thought—Jessica would have known for sure—swerved toward him, honking. He was walking on the wrong side of the road! He'd learned the words in kindergarten: "The left side is the right side, and the right side is suicide." He hadn't been contemplating suicide, but he could see why a summer on the island might make a person consider it.

Looking carefully both ways, he crossed to the other side of the road. His legs moved mechanically in a rhythm that was a drumbeat marking off the distance between him and the gestapo of Skyfield.

Even his escape was becoming boring because of the constant rain and because of the trees hemming him in on both sides. He slowed his pace for fifteen steps, increased it for fifteen, and slowed again. He tried jogging, then walking fast, then strolling. He was in his slow phase when he heard a car approaching from behind. It pulled up on the opposite shoulder of the road and stopped. It *was* a Ford Escort.

"Heading for the village?" A woman leaned out of the driver's window, smiling like the Happy Face that Mrs. Murphy, his first-grade teacher, used to paste on his finger paintings. "I'll give you a ride."

As he settled into the front seat beside the woman, he muttered a "Thanks" that sounded as soggy as he felt. She turned on the heater and warm air from the vent crept across his ankles and up his pant legs.

"You're an off-islander," she said. "One of the summer people." It didn't sound like a compliment.

"How did you know?" Trevor asked.

"No islander ever walks anywhere if he can help it. I suppose you're just out exploring?"

"Something like that."

"How far have you walked? You're wet as a lobster."

"Not far. I like walking in the rain." Trevor didn't think she believed him so he tried again. "It wasn't raining when I started." He didn't think she bought that one either. He watched the rain snake paths down his side window. A car came speeding around a curve and her questions stopped as she braked and steered closer to the edge of the narrow highway.

"I'll drop you off by the village post office, if that's where you want to go."

"Or maybe the bus station," he suggested as casually as he could.

"You must be really new to the island. We've got pickups and cars and bicycles and boats, but we don't do buses. You'd have to go clear over to Green Hill on the mainland to find one of those. There's a schedule on the bulletin board in the grocery store, though, if you like to read about buses." She was still chuckling when she pulled up at the edge of the village. "Guess it's the post office or nothing."

He had the door open almost before she came to a stop. "Thanks a lot for the ride. Maybe I'll go in and check out the Wanted posters."

"The best ones are over on the far wall. And no need for thanks." She was still smiling. "We'll see each other again. This isn't a very big island." It sounded a little like a threat.

He waited until she drove away, then looked around. Farther down the street a sign for Will's Groceries and Sundries stuck out above the sidewalk. He'd check out the bus schedule, and besides, the walk had left him starving.

It was no supermarket and it looked as old as everything else Trevor had seen on the island. The narrow aisles were cluttered with garden supplies and tools and slickers and rubber boots with groceries stuck in here and there among the rest. The schedule, when he finally found it, wasn't very encouraging. There was only one bus a week that went to Bangor. Still, that was better than nothing, he decided, pulling a bag of corn curls from a rack beside a stack of shotgun shells and arch supports.

At the checkout counter, Trevor waited while the man punched the price of corn curls on an old cash register that had a bell that jingled and a cash drawer that flew open. Trevor pulled a bill from his wallet and placed it on the counter.

"So you're Trevor Ackerman," the man remarked as if he were answering a question.

Trevor felt a shiver start at the base of his spine and work its way up to the back of his neck. The island might not be enchanted, but it must have a brain of its own that transmitted information to everyone who lived on it. "Yes, sir. How did you know?"

"Your Aunt Calla called to say she'd like you to pick up a loaf of stone-ground wheat bread. I'll put it in here and charge it to her account." He placed the bread and corn curls in a paper sack and handed it to Trevor. "Have a nice day," he added in a tired monotone.

Trevor started for the door. How had Aunt Cal known he would be in this store? He hadn't known it himself. Maybe his theory about the island-brain was fact.

"Oh, and Trevor," the man called. "She said to tell you your aunt Lou will be in to pick you up. You can wait out there on the bench. Looks like the rain has stopped."

"Thanks," Trevor mumbled. The island probably planned the weather, too—rain when he was walking, and now the clouds disappearing.

He sat down on the bench. Even with Aunt Cal locked in her library, he hadn't escaped Skyfield without her knowing he was gone. She might as well have planted a location detector in his pocket. He wasn't hungry anymore and it occurred to him that he hated corn curls anyway. He couldn't figure out why he'd bought them.

He automatically reached down to turn on the Walkman and then remembered that he'd run away in such a hurry that he'd left it on the bed. There was nothing to do while he waited but think.

Cars and pickups pulled to a stop by the post office, and people waved and called greetings to whoever happened to be around. Everyone seemed to know everybody else and to be happy to see them. He looked up into the sky, where clouds scudded seaward as if they couldn't leave fast enough.

He thought about the tomorrows he'd have to live through before he could leave Blue Isle if he couldn't get to Green Hill and catch a bus. This was like everything else in his life—stuff to be lived through so that he could get on to the next thing he was supposed to do: grade school, junior high, high school, college, Harvard Business School, where his father said Trevor would go.

He wondered where his future began. It must have started before he was born, before he even had a past. Now was now, though, something to be lived through before he got to a then that somebody else had planned for him.

He heard Lou's station wagon before he saw it creep by the post office and pull up at the curb in front of the store. Lou climbed out looking as if she'd come straight from the flower beds at Skyfield. She wore a droopy straw hat, faded blue jeans, and muddy rubber boots. Without saying a word, she walked over, sat on the bench beside him, and pulled off her work gloves.

Trevor wanted to say something, anything, but he couldn't even come up with a Freddie Ackerman thought.

His aunt pulled out a red bandanna, wiped her face, then tucked it back into her hip pocket. "If this rain keeps up, we'll all turn into mushrooms."

She already looked a little like one—brown and wrinkled—but that wasn't the sort of thing he could say out loud, so instead he reached for the grocery sack. "Want a corn curl?" he asked. Maybe if she was busy chewing she wouldn't start with questions about his trip into town.

"I love junk food!" She took the package and ripped it open. "Unfortunately, so does Calla, and it's all I can do to keep her on a cholesterol-free diet. Can't have anything like this in the house or she'd sniff it out in a minute. She has the instincts of a truffle hunter."

He'd eaten Aunt Cal's stash of goodies for breakfast! He watched as Lou popped two curls into her mouth, closed her eyes, and chewed slowly.

She swallowed, opened her eyes, and said, "Thank you, Trevor. You know, I was just reading about a man who had a dog that, he said, was so nearsighted it got lost on the end of its own leash." She took another handful of curls.

Trying to understand Lou was like decoding a secret document, but after a couple of minutes, he thought he knew what she meant. "I wasn't lost," he said. He waited for her to finish chewing.

"Of course not. You're here, aren't you? You inferred something that I didn't imply. And, as I told my sister, one can't draw a universal conclusion from two particulars. Don't you agree?"

"What particulars?" She'd lost him for sure this time.

She carefully closed the corn curl package, hesitated, opened it again and picked out two curls. "Calla knew you weren't in the house." She ate a curl. "I knew you hadn't taken the bicycle." She ate the other curl. "Conclusion: You had learned the art of levitation. And see how wrong we were? You were right here in the village waiting for me."

Trevor took a deep breath, opened his mouth, and then closed it.

Lou stood up suddenly and handed the package to Trevor. "They don't fill these the way they used to. Would you put it in the container over there? I have to pick up some plant fertilizer now that the rain has stopped."

On the slow drive back to Skyfield, neither he nor his aunt talked.

Freddie Ackerman, bound and gagged, was once again in the clutches of the secret police, silently vowing to find a way out of the dreaded citadel, even if it cost his life. He'd formulate his plans more carefully, for now he understood that the island itself was his enemy.

"How old did you say you were?" Lou asked as she parked the station wagon in front of the garage.

"Twelve."

"I suppose that's as good as any other age," she said thoughtfully, "but you could have more fun *being* it, you know." Then she shook her head. "No, you probably don't, or you would. Ten minutes till dinner, so we'll have to hurry!"

By the time Trevor washed, changed his clothes, and came downstairs, he'd figured out how to rearrange facts if the questions began. He'd say he'd wanted to mail a long letter to his mother telling her all about the plane trip and how interesting it was to be on Blue Isle. "When in doubt, lie," Jessica always said.

That wasn't necessary because as soon as he'd taken his seat at the table, Smiling Face appeared—the Sunshine Lady who'd given him a ride to the village.

"This is Melva," Aunt Cal explained as she took a serving dish from the woman. "Melva takes care of us. She comes each evening to cook, and she cleans once a week whether the house needs it or not."

"Trevor and I have met, although we forgot to introduce ourselves." Even her words came out smiling.

Trevor smiled, too, his lips feeling as if they were attached to his ears by rubber bands. He waited for someone to say, "And why were you so interested in the bus schedule?" No one did. Instead, Aunt Cal arranged chicken breasts and steamed broccoli on each of their plates and asked, "What do you think of the village now, after your tour?"

The only thing he hated more than fish was broccoli, but he tried to ignore the woody green things. "It was . . . pretty busy. A lot of people go to the post office."

"Must be the posters that draw them in," Melva said from the doorway.

Aunt Cal didn't seem to hear because she leaned toward him. "You've just arrived, and there is so much more to see." She extended an arm and gestured dramatically. " 'All the world's a stage,' " she intoned. "That's Shakespeare," she added, then picked up her fork and began eating very slowly, as if she were trying to convince herself that she liked what she was tasting.

Trevor stared at his plate. No lecture about how worried they'd been? No unanswerable questions? Not a single don't-ever-do-that-again-or-else? They weren't going to tell him he was grounded?

He stabbed at the chicken. Why would they bother to ground him when he was already stuck right up to his armpits on the edge of Blue Isle?

After dinner, on his way to his room, the last thing he heard was Aunt Cal's voice as she talked to Lou and Melva. "That boy will starve to death if we don't get some *real* food in this house. He won't be here long." It was quiet for a moment, until she added, "And don't look so righteous, Lou. Did you think I couldn't smell the corn curls on your breath?"

Trevor had never lived without rules before, and he

wasn't quite comfortable. How could he know for sure what he shouldn't do if there were no rules to break? Maybe he could make up some of his own, but he couldn't come up with anything he didn't want to do. The only thing he *wanted* to do was get to Green Hill and catch a bus. There wasn't even a rule against that.

The rain hadn't helped either. For a while he lost track of the days and didn't even remember what he'd done except turn on the lights in his bedroom, pretending the sun was shining. He would have made a run for Green Hill and the bus station, but he didn't have gills.

And then the sun burst through the clouds one day when Trevor had begun to think that he wouldn't just turn into a mushroom—he'd turn into green slime and slide away forever.

In the brightness of the morning sun, he forgot Green Hill, he forgot bus rides, he forgot that he was trapped. Instead, he ran out of the house, across the front lawn, and down toward the cove that curled in toward Skyfield. Feeling foolish, he stopped and looked back over his shoulder. No one had seen him. No faces were pressed against the windows. His aunts were as bored with him as he was with them. That should have made him feel better, but it didn't.

The cove, a smaller version of the bay beyond, curved in toward him, its shore dribbling off into a line of blackened rocks that ended in a lump of land floating on the water. On one edge of the tiny island, a shaggy tree towered like a giant umbrella.

Before he had time to think, his feet were moving him toward the shoreline and then to a faint path that cut off into the trees toward the line of rock Trevor had seen from the lawn.

Freddie Ackerman moved on soundless feet through the forest, thinking of his men back on the tiny fishing smack, off the French coast. If he did not return by dawn, they would set sail for England. Good men and true, they would obey his final orders.

Hand on his pistol, he made his shadowlike way among the trees until he reached the boulders, smooth and sun-dried. Stepping carefully, he balanced as he made his way to a ledge that led to the island itself. Clambering up, he kissed the earth and spoke. "For the flag, and for me, Captain Freddie Ackerman, I claim this—Lost Island."

He felt a wet splat on his shoulder and looked up. A single gull swept away across the water. Trevor pulled off his T-shirt, wiped it on the scraggy grass, and propped himself against the trunk of the big tree. He didn't bother to turn on his Walkman. The batteries were fading and all he could hear was a dull buzz. He'd have to replace them. Even so, he felt more comfortable with the earphones clasping his neck.

He looked out across the bay at the fine line where sky met water. It was almost frightening to know that the cove opened up into the bay, and the bay into the ocean, and the ocean into the world. He wondered how many rivers it took to fill all the oceans and why seawater was salty when the rivers weren't.

Maybe it was the sound of water lapping against the rocks, or maybe it was the sad crying of the gulls, but something made him remember how he used to pretend he owned an ancient treasure chest. It was covered with golden dragons and opened with a solid-gold key.

Inside, he kept his Forever Things—things he loved to think about, like Miss Erdman, his third-grade teacher who really cared about him; Tinker, the kitten he had until she was run over; Bub Jackson, who was his best friend until the Jacksons moved to New Jersey. Trevor had stopped storing things when Norman came.

He stretched out on his stomach and made a pillow of his arms. He thought about writing a letter to his mother when he went back to the house, but there was nothing to say. He considered putting a note in a bottle and throwing it into the cove. He'd write, "I'm the real Freddie Ackerman. *Help!*" He didn't have a bottle, though.

He turned over on his back and stared up at the sky. It was strange to think of all those stars and galaxies looking down on him, even now in the daytime when he couldn't see them. He closed his eyes and dived back into himself and listened to the sound of his heart beating.

When he was a little kid he pretended he had a brother named Lark. Lark always sat beside him on the same chair at the dinner table. That annoyed Trevor's father, who insisted Trevor move over in his chair and "sit up straight like a little man." Lark never cared, though, and when Trevor was sent to his room for forgetting a rule,

Lark went along. Sometimes Lark misbehaved, too, and drew crayon pictures on the bedroom walls. He was good at making up stories about ghosts and witches that were so real he frightened himself, but Trevor protected him and kept him from crying.

The day Trevor's mother said that his father wasn't going to live with them anymore and that Trevor had to be the man of the family, Lark disappeared.

"Lark! Come and find me," he called from the darkness behind his eyes. He listened, but no one answered.

Trevor was floating in a still darkness, a soft, velvety darkness that covered him like a blanket of feathers. Then he was swimming in sea-blue water, arching like a dolphin into silver waves and leaving a wake of sparkles behind.

In the middle of a dream in which he was caught in an underwater room with no doors or windows and filled with books, he heard someone call his name.

He struggled to answer, but his mouth wouldn't work.

"Trevor!" the voice repeated, clearer now.

It was Lark. "Come back, Lark. I'm right here." The words came out in a funny, garbled mumble that sounded strange even to him.

"Trevor, can you hear me?"

He sat up. It wasn't Lark; it was Aunt Cal's booming voice. He scrambled to his feet, rubbed his eyes, and looked toward Skyfield. Aunt Cal stood at the edge of the lawn, arms folded across her chest, and beside her, Lou paced back and forth.

"Here I am," he said, waving. The wave became a weak flap when he saw that the big rocks that lined Skyfield's shore had disappeared and the water of the cove came right up to the grass. He glanced back at the boulders he'd climbed to get to the island. At first, he didn't believe what he saw, so he didn't think he saw it. The stones were nowhere in sight, and water lapped at the edge of the island.

"What should I do?" he shouted.

"Stay where you are!" Aunt Cal's voice sounded much farther away than she looked. "Homer will come get you."

He didn't know who Homer was, and he didn't care. Trevor could swim, sort of, but he wasn't sure how far. At camp he cheated by hanging on to the side of the pool for an extra breath or two. In the cove, there was nothing to hang on to.

His aunts had binoculars now and were watching him, so he tried to look confident. If he ever did get back to shore, they'd probably send him away on the first flight out, after they finished yelling at him for being so stupid. He'd known there were tides, of course, and that they came in highs and lows, but how long and how high? With each new push, water crept nearer.

Freddie Ackerman stood on the bridge of his PT boat as the deck trembled under his feet. His crew was safe, their life raft almost out of sight on the darkening sea. He smiled grimly. Mission completed! The enemy destroyer had sunk beneath the waves of the North Atlantic; he was content now to confront the ultimate enemy—death itself!

Around a bend in the shore, a uniformed man slowly propelled a weather-beaten rowboat that looked as if it might capsize with every stroke of the oars.

"You'll be fine now, Trevor," Aunt Cal called.

Trevor was not convinced. He could hear the words on "Eyewitness News": "Abandoned boy swept out to sea by tidal wave!" He wondered if his mom and Charlie had time to watch TV in Bermuda. Actually, though, if he did drown, it would solve a lot of problems. Could his aunts cash in his plane ticket? They could probably use the money.

He was sure the water never really covered Lost Island; otherwise, nothing would be able to grow. Still, he wished the man would row a little harder and move a little faster, even if he might be safer on the island than in a leaky boat.

Finally, with a pull on one oar that Trevor thought might catapult the man into the cove, the man nudged the rowboat up against the rocks. "Slide down on your stomach, feet first, and try to hit the middle of the boat." He was wearing a police uniform, complete with badge. Trevor's aunts were going to have him arrested for trespassing!

Even that was better than drowning, so he slipped over the rocky edge and landed wetly in the bottom of the boat.

"I didn't know . . ." Trevor started to explain. "I mean about the tide. I didn't mean to . . ."

"Off-islander," the man said, sounding bored. "Happens every summer. Too dang lazy to read the tide charts, all of you. Better learn how."

Either the man was out of breath, or he thought whole sentences were a waste of words, but Trevor had a more important question to ask. "How mad are my aunts?"

"*I'm* the one doing all the work. 'Just call old Homer.' Cat up a tree, electricity on the blink, car don't start, summer people need saving, 'Just call old Homer.' Besides, they're too level-headed to be mad." He paused a minute and added, "I think."

Huddled in the boat, wet from the waist down, Trevor hoped that his aunts would *keep* their heads level.

Homer let the tide carry them up to the shore, and Trevor crawled out. As he walked across the lawn, water squished between his toes. He hurried to explain before his aunts had a chance to talk. "I did something really stupid, didn't I?" Jessica said it was best to blame yourself before someone else did.

It must have worked because Lou's voice wasn't angry when she said, "No. There's a difference between stupidity and ignorance. Ignorance makes one mistake; stupidity makes the same mistake twice. Now I've got to get back to work."

Aunt Cal walked toward him, her red-and-gold caftan whirling in the breeze. Trevor felt as if he'd suddenly shrunk to Munchkin size.

"Were you afraid?" She sounded like his shrink when she was being curious about his dreams.

"Sort of," he admitted, hoping for sympathy.

She looked at him, starting with his sneakers and ending somewhere just above his eyebrows. "Sensible. You weren't in any real danger, but you'd have had a long, lonely time waiting for the tide to recede."

"I thought about swimming back . . ."

"You were wise not to have tried. The cove is deep and the water is cold, as you might have noticed." She glanced down at his sodden pants and motioned him toward the house.

He couldn't figure her out. She said he was *wise* not to try to swim; his mother or Other-Mother-Daphne would have pointed out how stupid it was for him even to consider the idea. On the other hand, Aunt Cal probably didn't care *what* he did, as long as he didn't get killed.

"I'm sorry you had to call the police, though. I think he was really mad." Trevor hoped it sounded like a sincere apology.

"Homer? He loves to complain, but he doesn't mean a word of it. He just gets upset because there's no real crime on Blue Isle. The only reasons he doesn't retire are his uniform and his police car and the chance to sound official in front of summer people."

Trevor figured that as long as he could keep her talking, she wouldn't have time to decide that having him around was more trouble than he was worth. He was going to leave—that was sure—but he didn't want to be *sent*. He tried another question. "Does the little island belong to you?"

"If it belongs to anyone, it belongs to the lovers." She stopped and looked back toward the cove.

"Lovers?" The words sounded so funny coming from Aunt Cal that he almost laughed.

"Local legend says that long ago an Indian couple were killed on the little island trying to run away together. They were from rival tribes. Two trees grew over their grave, two trees that entwine as one."

If she believed that, she'd believe anything. "I've heard that kind of story before. But in Iowa, her name was Wapsie and his name was Pinicon, and they drowned in a river that's called Wapsipinicon. It's not really true."

Aunt Cal opened the porch door. "Perhaps not, but I prefer living in a world where such things *could* happen. Myth is so much more interesting than truth. I suppose that you are too grown-up to agree." She shooed him through the door. "Run along and get cleaned up. You've missed lunch, such as it was, but I'm sure you can find something in the refrigerator. You really must give me that food list, or I'll have to make up one of my own."

He hurried to his room, trying not to drip on the stairs. She was just like all the rest of the adults in his life. One minute she said he was grown-up and the next minute she was treating him like a little kid, and the rest of the time he was supposed to magically disappear.

Jessica had been right when she said that twelve-year-olds were an endangered species.

Five down and eighty-nine days to go! Caught behind enemy lines and now in solitary confinement, Major Freddie Ackerman huddled over the tiny heat vent as cold rain lashed the isolated German castle. From some distant room, he heard his captors' voices as they planned his fate.

It wasn't raining on Blue Isle; instead, a cold, clammy fog brushed against the windows. Still in pajamas, with a blanket draped around his shoulders, Trevor huddled over the old-fashioned floor register in his bedroom while his aunts talked in the kitchen below.

"He's more trouble than he's worth." Aunt Cal's voice burst up through the grating.

He leaned closer. Were they talking about him?

"To tell the truth, Louisa, he takes up space," she went on. "Don't you think he has to go?"

Go? They wanted to get rid of him already?

"You think so?" Lou didn't sound as if she cared.

"I've tried everything I know, and it's just wasted effort. I can't see much point in postponing the inevitable." Aunt Cal's voice was flat.

Trevor sat up straight. He didn't want to hear any more, but then he got down on all fours and pressed an ear against the register.

"I thought he'd improved," Lou said.

"Not that I can see. I'm beginning to think it's a genetic weakness, like a bad seed."

Lou laughed. "Maybe we should try talking to him."

"Talking?" Aunt Cal laughed, too. "If you ask me, it would be a waste of perfectly good words. I don't feel guilty about the decision, mind you. As the old Greek poet said, 'If this be crime, the crime's confessed.' "

"It's up to you, Calla." A chair scraped on the tile floor. "Whatever you say is all right. It just means another trip for me."

"I suppose we can wait a little longer. We'll try a bit more support. After all, there's no one else who'd want him."

Trevor didn't move. He couldn't. It was one thing for *him* to wish he was someplace else; it was awful to have his aunts wish the same thing.

Freddie Ackerman knew exactly what had to be done. He'd hock his Walkman and buy a bus ticket to Bangor; he'd change his plane ticket for . . . He could figure that out when he got to the airport.

It didn't take long to dress and stuff some clothes and what was left of his money, along with his plane ticket, into his backpack. He secured the Walkman on his belt and waited till he heard his aunts leave the kitchen. On his way out of the house, he paused long enough to grab a couple of apples and some diet Coke from the refrigerator. He felt a little guilty about never making out the list of food Aunt Cal hoped for.

The bicycle she had mentioned that first night was a one-speed, pink, girl's Schwinn. It had balloon tires and must have been as old as his aunts, but it was wheels.

He shivered as he pedaled down the drive, the tops of trees hidden in the fog. By the time he got to the main road, he wished he hadn't worn the extra sweatshirt with Meeker School Sucks printed on it.

Soon he was across the causeway and over the bridge. Freddie Ackerman coasted at top speed, his pursuers far behind. He glanced over his shoulder. Someone was gaining on him! It was time to pedal his fastest. He sped around a wide curve that revealed the end of the French Alps looming ahead. Only a few more grueling miles and then—Paris.

Trevor was getting tired. The fog was gone and the sun was hot. The road climbed and fell like a never-ending roller coaster. On one hill, he gave up and got off to walk, pushing the heavy bike. Halfway up he considered turning around, but when he reached the top, he changed his mind. When he started up the next hill that stretched so far he couldn't see the top, he stopped to rest. Off the road, he shrugged out of his backpack and slumped in the shade of a tree.

Adjusting the earphones of his Walkman, he leaned back and relaxed. He'd forgotten his watch. Other-Father-Norman had spent a great part of one Saturday afternoon trying to explain how to tell time by facing north and looking at his shadow. It hadn't made sense, and the sun was so high now, Trevor didn't know where north was.

He picked up a pine needle and broke it into tiny pieces. He wondered what his real dad was doing. If it was eleven o'clock here, it would be seven in California, and his dad would probably be coming down for breakfast, already dressed in a three-piece suit and carrying his brief-case. Maybe he slept with his briefcase.

You didn't have any choice when it came to parents. Being stuck with two unchosen ones was enough. Who needed as many as he had?

Trevor ate one apple but he was still thirsty, so he finished the other cola. He'd save the second apple for the bus station.

He stared up at the trees. Jessica said trees were magic, and that they heard everything, even thoughts, and could remember when they were cut up for lumber. "That's why when the wind blows you hear the house creak. It's the trees remembering and telling secrets to each other."

He usually knew when Jessica believed what she said, but when it came to trees, he wasn't too sure.

He turned up the volume on his Walkman. Rap or funk or retooled metal or anything with a strong backbeat could turn off his brain for hours. His eyes glazed as his ears filled with the sound of his kind of music.

He had no idea how long he'd been listening when he finally pulled off the earphones. A car roared down the hill, whizzed by with a blast of wind, and gradually faded away into a lonely hum.

He'd never get to the bus station at this rate. He shrugged into his backpack and started up the long hill, pushing the bike. The farther he went, the harder the Schwinn was to push. He moved to the shoulder of the road and flipped down the kickstand, then glanced at the back tire.

It was no longer a balloon. He didn't know how far he'd come. He was sure, though, as he looked down at the tire, squashed and wrinkled, that he'd have to go back to Skyfield, whether his aunts wanted him or not. He started back down the hill, walking and guiding the bike.

He didn't hear her until she spoke. "Flat tire?" Raspy, her voice sounded as if she might have a cold.

It was such a stupid question. "Just on the bottom," he growled.

"Where are you taking it?"

"Home." He couldn't believe he'd said the word. He glanced over at the girl. Her hair was the color of straw. She had green eyes, a face full of freckles, and eyebrows—which at first he didn't think she had—the same straw color as her hair.

"I know somebody who'd fix it for you."

He didn't answer. The last thing he needed was a flat tire. The *next*-to-the-last was this girl and her suggestions.

"Won't cost too much, either." She scuffed along beside him like an unwanted puppy.

"Who'd fix it?"

"Me!" She skipped on ahead, turned around, and walked backward so that he had to look straight at her. "For three bucks. Do you have three bucks?"

"Sure," he answered. He had four, but he wouldn't tell her that, or she'd probably raise her price.

"We'll have to take it to my place, though. It's down at the bottom of the hill and over on that other road. Want to go?"

Riding the bike would be easier than pushing it. "I guess so. Why not?"

"Here, then let me take it." She grabbed the handlebars from him and started running down the hill.

"Hey, wait a minute!" He ran to catch up with her. He wouldn't have been surprised if she'd darted off into the woods with Aunt Cal's antique wheels, leaving him stranded.

"What's your name?" she shouted back at him.

He caught up to her and pulled the handlebars away. "What's yours?"

"Ariel." She stopped and planted both feet in front of the bicycle. "Don't you dare say 'TV aerial.' "

"I wasn't going to." She wasn't very big, but what there was of her was packed so firmly that he didn't want to make her mad.

"I'll bet you thought it!" She was glaring at him as if he'd actually said it.

"I did not. An ariel's a kind of gazelle, isn't it?"

"What's a gazelle?" She stepped aside and let him continue wheeling the Schwinn down the hill.

"It's an animal, a kind of deer. I saw one on television." Just in case she thought it was an insult, he added, "A very pretty animal."

She stopped scowling. "Kids at school call me Mickey."

"I like Ariel better." Maybe she'd drop the price.

Ariel led him to a road that wound off among more trees—not just a wood, but a forest that a person could get lost in. They finally came to a clearing where an unpainted lean-to was attached to a skinny mobile home that looked as if it hadn't been mobile for a long time. The place wasn't exactly junky; it looked tired. Ariel took the bike, wheeled it to the shed, and began pulling out tools as if she knew what she was doing.

"Are you home alone?" From the way she was attacking the bike, he could almost believe she lived here by herself.

"Grandpa's inside, sleeping."

"Is that who you live with?"

"Part-time." Already she had the wheel yanked from the frame and was prying the tire from the rim. "Mom works in Bangor, so I stay here in the summer."

"What does your dad do?" He wasn't sure why he was asking. Maybe because he'd been trapped with old people for so long, it felt good to talk to a real person, a kid his own age.

"I don't have one. I never did." She pulled the rubbery insides out of the tire. Trevor hadn't known bike tires had insides.

He hunched down and held the tire as she pulled on the tube. "Everybody has to have a dad. I have three."

She frowned at him. "All at the same time?"

"Not exactly." He wished he hadn't mentioned them. "Then did they die?"

He decided to tell the truth. "No, Mom just likes getting married."

Ariel held up the inner tube. "Look. It's a puncture. See?" She pointed at a tiny spot no bigger than a fleck of dust.

"Are you sure you know what you're doing?" Aunt Cal's bike was upside down in the middle of the shed, its empty back wheel leaning against the wall, the tire sagging beside it.

"Do you think you could do better?" She didn't wait for an answer. "I have to get some more stuff. Don't go away." She ran out the door.

Where did she think he'd be going? He was hot, sweaty, hungry, thirsty, tired, and generally miserable. The bike was in pieces and if Airhead Ariel couldn't put it back together, he'd be trapped right here for the rest of the summer.

He tried not to think of what would be waiting if he ever got back to Skyfield. This, along with everything else, would send him straight to the *its* in Southern California. He'd have to come up with a really convincing story to explain where he'd been all day, in order to get another chance to leave under his own power.

"I'm back," Ariel announced as she knelt and spread out the contents of a repair kit: a tube of transparent glue, rubber patches of all sizes and shapes, a pair of scissors, and some sandpaper. "You belong to Miss Louisa and Miss Calla, don't you?" she asked as she picked up the inner tube and started buffing it gently with the sandpaper.

"I don't belong to anybody," Trevor said. "I'm just staying there for a few weeks. Anyway, how did you know?"

"I recognized the bike, and besides, my aunt Melva works for them. I even knew your name. I just pretended I didn't. Is the house really filled with books? Boy, are you lucky!"

The last thing he wanted to talk about was Skyfield and books. "Are you sure you're fixing that thing?" Maybe she was ruining the tube with all her sanding and scratching.

"Look, just because I'm a girl . . ."

"Oh, I didn't mean that! I meant, where did you learn?"

"From Grandpa. He knows how to fix everything. He runs the mail boat." She stopped sanding and began spreading a thin coat of glue on the inner tube.

"Your grandfather is a mailman?"

"Boy, are you dumb!" She leaned so close he could see that she really *did* have eyebrows. "He's *captain* of the mail boat that goes to the other islands. He gets up really early in the mornings and that's why he's sleeping now." Ariel went back to work on the tube. "Where were you going when you got the flat?"

"No place special. I was just riding around." It didn't sound very convincing. "Maybe over to that town— Green Hill."

"You really are dumb! That's another twenty miles, and it's all uphill. So how long are you going to stay at Skyfield?"

He wanted to tell her she'd better ask his aunts. "I'm not sure." Why didn't she stop asking questions he didn't want to answer? Looking like a pudgy Buddha, she was sitting cross-legged on the floor, tucking the inner tube back into the tire.

"Do you have brothers and sisters?"

"More or less." She *did* know what she was doing! She had the tire back on its rim and was dragging out an old tire pump from under the workbench.

"What do you mean?"

"I have more and I'd like less." He watched as she pumped air into the tire. "I have some halves and some steps. Some are boys and some are girls."

"You must live in a really big house."

"I don't live with any of them. We're not a family."

"There," she said, as if she hadn't heard him. "I told you I could fix it." She set the bike upright.

Trevor reached into his backpack. "Did you say three dollars?"

"I guess." Ariel looked around as if she'd forgotten something. "Two dollars is enough. It was a small puncture."

"Okay, then. Two dollars." He held out the bills.

She brushed past him and began to pick up the tools. "Make it one dollar. It was a *tiny* puncture."

"What difference does that make? What size the puncture is?"

She stood with her back to him, stuffing tools into the repair kit. "Because . . ." she began, then lowered her voice so that he could hardly hear. "There wasn't any puncture. I just pretended there was—to get you to talk to me."

"The tire *was* flat!" Trevor walked toward her, so close he could see her neck bobble when she swallowed.

She turned and ran toward the door. "I let the air out of your tire when you were listening to your Walkman. You had your eyes closed."

"What did you do that for?" he shouted after her. "You didn't have to. I'd have talked to you anyway. Honest!" The screen door of the mobile home slammed shut behind her.

He stood for a moment, not knowing whether to leave or to wait and see if she came back. What a dork! Going to all that trouble just to get someone to talk to her. Nobody could be that lonesome.

When he finally decided that Ariel wasn't going to reappear, he put three one-dollar bills under the repair kit. If he managed to hock his Walkman, he wouldn't need the money anyway. Too bad she didn't have any friends, but at least she didn't have three fathers and two mothers to shuffle her around.

A couple of hours later, he pedaled the Schwinn slowly up the drive toward Skyfield, his legs so numb they could have belonged to someone else.

Lou met him at the end of the drive.

"I had a flat tire," Trevor began the explanation he'd been planning. "I had it fixed, though, and it only cost three dollars."

As they walked together toward the house, Lou looked over at him. "Do you always take your backpack when you go for a bike ride? Of course I know you couldn't move without that thing." She pointed at the Walkman. "You've had a long day, but I told Calla not to worry, that you could take care of yourself."

"Was she afraid that I couldn't?" It was an interesting idea.

Lou opened the back door. "No. She was afraid you could."

It didn't make any more sense than most of the things his aunts said, but being back at Skyfield wasn't so bad after all.

Staying at Skyfield *was* like trying to balance on a sagging tightwire, because by the next morning his aunts didn't act as if they were going to get rid of him. They didn't try to "straighten him up" or give him "support" either.

Aunt Cal hurried past him with a fast "good morning," and Lou had already vanished. Maybe, overnight, they'd forgotten about yesterday. They *were* awfully old.

Trevor's legs were still sore from his long bike ride and he needed to really get in shape before he tried the trip to Green Hill again. He wouldn't push his luck— he'd stay close to Skyfield and be a model great-nephew for a while.

THE TIDE WAS out, and in the cove, the boulders leading to Lost Island lay exposed like beached whales. Trevor followed the pebbled shoreline to where the cove became part of the bay itself. A path angled away from the water and wound off into a mass of dark firs.

On Blue Isle, a path didn't have many places to lead. Trevor didn't care. It was a good day for following a trail that went nowhere. A few steps into the woods and the trees closed behind him, blotting out the shore. Spruce grew straight and tall, the ground beneath littered with needles.

Major General Freddie Ackerman, disguised in the uniform of a private, moved like a shadow through the Black Forest. Behind him, he heard the dogs! The guards from the stalag were closing in as light and shadow flickered on the forest floor.

Something rustled in the bushes behind him and Trevor moved faster. Just when he was thinking of turning back, the path sloped up, trees parted, and he was standing at the edge of a clearing.

A crumbling foundation of a house lay half-buried in grass and weeds, and behind it stood a gray building that might once have been a stable. It had that kind of door—split across the middle so that it could be opened from top or bottom. Since the path led directly to the door, he walked over, pulled open the top half, and looked in.

Trevor was positive the month was June. He was sure he was on Blue Isle. But he knew he was looking at the closest thing to Santa's workshop between Maine and the North Pole.

A potted pine tree decorated with Christmas ornaments, silver icicles, and hundreds of tiny lights stood in one corner, with brightly wrapped packages scattered beneath. Across the room, a miniature town, complete with Santa and reindeer on a rooftop, spread across the floor. Christmas cards, stapled to ribbons of green and red, dangled from the ceiling.

Trevor opened the lower half of the door, walked in, and sat down in a swivel chair next to a worktable. He tried to convince himself that all this was left over from the time people lived in the house next door that wasn't there anymore.

"So you found my cell. I wondered how long it would take."

Trevor whirled around so quickly that he almost spun himself out of the chair.

Lou leaned against the open doorway, arms crossed, a backpack like his slung over one shoulder. "As my sister would say, 'If you be pleased, retire into my cell and there repose.' That's Shakespeare."

"Sure," he hurried to agree, scrambling to his feet. "I didn't touch anything. The door wasn't locked."

"This is Blue Isle. We don't lock doors." She pulled a yellow legal pad and some pens from her pack, tossed them onto the table, and sat down. "So what do you think of it?" She waved her hand around the room.

"It's different." Trevor hesitated. "Isn't it a little late for Christmas?"

"Among many other things, Trevor, Christmas is a state of mind. In my case it is a statement of my mind. At least it had better be before the end of the month."

"I don't understand," he said, thinking that was the biggest understatement he'd ever made.

"Simple, really. I need it this way for my work." Lou reached down and turned on a switch that set the tree lights blinking.

"What work?"

"I scribble." Trevor must have looked as blank as his mind felt because after a moment of complete silence, Lou went on patiently. "I write poems, if you can call them that, for greeting-card companies. Messages for the masses—versatile verses of sympathy, empathy, anniversaries, birthdays—"

"And Christmas," Trevor finished her sentence. "You mean real people write that stuff?"

"Where did you think it sprang from?"

"Computers, maybe," Trevor suggested.

Lou nodded slowly and said thoughtfully, "I suppose they could, but if they did, a lot of us real people would have to find honest work."

"Why all this?" Trevor pointed at the Christmas tree.

"I need to work six months in advance," Lou went on. "That means I write about Christmas in June, which is not easy to do. All this, as you call it, is meant to put me in the mood to crank out ninety-five Christmas thoughts by the end of this month."

Trevor looked around the room again. She did make some kind of warped sense. "You need a fan with a big chunk of ice in front of it, or better yet, an air conditioner."

Lou seemed to consider his suggestion, then picked up a pen and squared the legal pad in front of her. "It's a good idea, but right now I don't need to cool down. I need to warm up. You don't mind some music, I hope." She reached over and flipped a tape player on. "You're welcome to stay as long as you can stand it."

Trevor perched on the arm of a broken-down couch and watched Lou as Bing Crosby started dreaming of a white Christmas. The way she gripped the pen and stared at the yellow paper looked as if she expected words to jump onto the page for her.

He let himself slide off the arm and onto the couch,

the sagging springs groaning. It was hard to believe that Lou and Aunt Cal were really sisters when they looked and acted so different. Aunt Cal was big, billowing, and bellowing sometimes, yet she looked as soft as a down-filled pillow. Lou was little and crisp and always moving, even when she was sitting still.

Trevor crossed his arms under his head, trying to get comfortable. It was kind of nice—being with someone—even if she'd forgotten he was there. All he could hear was the gentle swish of the wind outside and the occasional scratch of Lou's pen. Something made him think of his mom, but when he tried to remember her face, he couldn't. He couldn't remember Charlie's face either, but that was okay.

Lou sighed, flipped her legal pad over to a new page, and stared at the Christmas tree. One tape ended and now somebody was singing about being home for Christmas. That was what was wrong with Christmas. Trevor was never sure which parent's turn it would be to have him unless he wrote it down somewhere. Jessica said he was lucky because he ended up with twice as many presents that way. Sometimes, Jessica didn't understand how he felt.

Lou shoved her chair away from the table. "Too much is sometimes enough," she said, tearing off several sheets of paper, crumpling them, and tossing them into the wastebasket.

"Did you finish?" Trevor asked.

"I'm never finished! After Christmas, it's Valentine's

Day, then Easter. June has graduations and weddings. . . ." She stood and tucked her pad and pen into the backpack. "Cards stretch on to eternity, an endless river of drivel." She stopped moving. "River of drivel," she repeated, shaking her head. "See? After dreaming up perfectly awful ideas, I can't even speak in normal English."

Trevor started to get up from the couch.

"No need to leave. Stay as long as you want," she announced as she left. "Just turn off everything when you go. I've had enough brain drain for one afternoon."

Trevor waited until she got to the path before he scrounged the crumpled yellow pages from the trash basket. For one moment, he felt a little guilty, but by the time he'd smoothed out the paper, his guilt had disappeared as quickly as his aunt had.

It took a little while to decipher the scrawl of her writing.

> Under the blossom that hangs on the bough
>   Shines my special Christmas vow:
> For you on this festive day of the year,
>   The merriest of Christmas cheer!

It wasn't too bad—at least it rhymed. He looked at the other beginnings.

> Under the bright star
> Under the holly

Under the mistletoe
Under the baubles
Under the bloody lights

Was that the way to write poetry? He read on.

Yule log many miles
Before Yule learn
That home is the place
Where true Yules burn.

Trevor was about to wad up the paper when he saw a last poem squeezed down in the lower left-hand corner of the page.

What in the world, whatever
Shall we conceivably do with Trevor?
No matter how much we endeavor,
He remains so impossibly clever!

He wasn't sure whether he should be angry or pleased. He'd never found himself in a poem before. Of course, he hadn't read any poems since his Mother Goose days, but he was positive there were no Trevors in any of them.

He smoothed the paper to get rid of the creases, folded it carefully, and stuck it in his shirt pocket. He bet Jessica had never had a poem written about her, but there weren't many words that rhymed with Jessica. Maybe when the summer was over and when he got home and if he was speaking to her, he'd show it to her—casually, as if he were written about all the time by published poets like Lou.

Trevor shut off all the switches, closed both the top and bottom doors, and started back to Skyfield, feeling he might be someone he liked very much.

"SEVENTY-NINE. EIGHTY."

Trevor did the last push-up and scrambled to his feet. Not bad—two minutes faster than the day before, and he was almost positive that, after just a few days, his muscles were bigger. Not much, maybe, but if he kept it up, Jessica could never say again what she'd said that day in the hall.

He didn't bother to make up his bed. His aunts wouldn't come in to check. Other-Mother-Daphne insisted that he make his bed every morning. "Pull the sheets tight! Smooth the coverlet flat! Be sure to hang up your towel and washcloth." Absolute neatness paid off with her, and it was also a sure way to tell if the *its* had been pawing through his things.

He looked at his rumpled bed. Not doing things made him feel in control.

In the kitchen, he found a candy bar tucked inside a fat-free cheese wrapper. He didn't even feel guilty stealing it from Aunt Cal. He'd handed her a list of food that had sent her eyebrows up to her hairline and turned her face into one large smile.

"Trevor"—she materialized through the doorway—"I have some errands to run on the mainland. . . ."

It was hard to imagine her running anywhere.

"You might like to come along. I could use your help."

How many different caftans did she have? They were all shaped the same way, but he'd counted at least a dozen different colors. Today's was purple, and she reminded him of a giant, ripe plum.

"Sure," he said, still looking at her outfit. "Shall I change my clothes?"

"Don't bother. This is business plus a little grocery shopping. Not very exciting, I'm afraid. Except for the groceries."

He followed her outside, feeling as if he should be picking up her train. He expected the station wagon. Instead, Aunt Cal magically oozed in behind the wheel of a British-racing-green Miata with license plates that spelled out MS CAL. So that's why they had a two-car garage.

"Some machine!" he said, fastening his seat belt.

Her laughter rumbled as they whipped out of the driveway. "You wouldn't expect me to drive that monster of your aunt's, would you? It'll be the death of her yet. Now, to the post office."

The trip was much faster with Aunt Cal than with Lou, because she straightened out all the curves instead of yanking the car around them.

THE POST OFFICE was small, one wall lined with rows of glass-fronted boxes, dials on the front of each. Trevor watched his aunt spin the dial of one around and back and around again until the glass door opened. A counter ran along another wall, and as Aunt Cal sorted through the mail, Miss Florence, the postmistress, filled her in on everything that had happened on Blue Isle in the last twenty-four hours.

Aunt Cal piled her own correspondence in one stack, Lou's in another, and handed Trevor the magazines, newspapers, and junk mail. The only thing he ever received was a card from his mother once a week, and all of them looked the same—pink beaches and palm trees.

"The mainland next," Aunt Cal announced once they were back in the car and speeding across hills and valleys, downshifting on the sharp curves. She drove with one hand on the wheel, the other on the gearshift.

"Look back, Trevor. Isn't it spectacular the way Blue Isle seems to drop off into the Bay?"

"Spectacular," he breathed, as the ugly blob of green that was Blue Isle disappeared from his view.

Aunt Cal smiled. Freddie Ackerman rolled his eyes.

"We'll stop at the grocery store first. Scrabble season begins tonight—a wonderful excuse to buy human food. And thank you for *your* list, by the way. Now there will be plenty of snacks around."

"Am I supposed to play Scrabble?" He hated board games, especially if they involved words.

"Oh, no. Our tournament consists of Dirk and Celia— they own Pilgrim's Inn—and Melva and one of her friends. We've been playing for years."

She made it sound like the fight to get to the Super Bowl. Maybe his aunts were too old to know the difference between a Scrabble tournament and real fun. Maybe they'd been together for so long that doing anything with other people was exciting.

"Have you and Lou always lived together?" He couldn't imagine how long "always" was.

"Certainly not!" She sounded amazed. "When we were younger, we led quite separate lives." She smiled and added, "We didn't always approve of each other. Sometimes we still don't."

"Do you like each other? I mean you don't *have* to live together, do you?" The only reason he could imagine for staying together so long was what his mother called "economic expediency."

"We do, indeed, like each other. Just because we're sisters doesn't mean we can't be friends, and because we're friends, we can be ourselves. Louisa is a bit odd, I grant you. . . ."

She slowed the car and turned in to the supermarket parking lot. "But then I suppose I am, too." She turned off the ignition. "So are you, young man, if I might add, which is all to the good. Do you understand what I'm saying?"

"I think so. I have a friend who . . ." He was going to tell her about Jessica, except Jessica wasn't his friend anymore.

"That's wonderful, Trevor," she said. "Everyone should have a friend. Now, do you want to come with me or stay in the car?"

"I'll stay here."

He watched his aunt march through the automatic door of the market as he settled back to wait. She certainly drove one sweet car. He ran his hand along the steering wheel. He could almost feel what it would be like to take the curves of Blue Isle in a flash of green and glistening chrome.

He riffled through the mail, knowing there was nothing for him. At least he didn't have to go in and push a stupid cart up and down aisles while she stood and peered at shelves. He hated doing that, especially if he was with Other-Mother-Daphne and the *its*, who took turns hopping off the cart and grabbing stuff from display racks.

He pulled out one of Aunt Cal's magazines. There were hardly any pictures in it, just column after column of words. He flipped to the back and began reading the classified advertisements. At least they were short.

Tired of friends who don't write?
Eager for thoughtful communication?
Meet women worldwide. Free address list.

He wondered if they'd send pictures too. Jessica had a picture of her pen pal.

Noted philosopher gives advice on personal problems. Call for details.

There was a twenty-four-hour-a-day phone number.

Talk with Sister Linus Psychic Reader. She knows your inner heart and will help you discover yourself. You can be more than you dream. Phone readings.

CONFIDENTIAL: Meet lovely ladies or gentlemen— worldwide or next door.

Every listing had a coupon to fill out or a phone number to call. He was about to start looking through the next magazine when Aunt Cal emerged from the store, followed by a kid with his arms full of grocery sacks. If the Scrabblers could finish all that food, Trevor didn't see how they'd have time to play many games. Maybe that was why Aunt Cal liked Scrabble.

"Business next," she said when they finally got underway. "I need to pick up some books from a house in town. You can help me carry."

"You want more books?" Her library was already full. Why didn't she read some of them again instead of getting more?

"These came from an estate auction. They've been in the house for generations and no one looked at them for years. I came across a couple of special ones along with a box or two of goodness-knows-what that I'll probably have to dispose of. It's like looking for buried treasure. I never know what I might find."

She must really need money if the only books she bought were already used.

They pulled up in front of a series of steps that led to a house perched on a grassy knoll—a house that looked like three or four houses pushed together with porches in between.

"Once I found some books at a farm auction not too far from here," Aunt Cal said as they climbed the steps. "When I got home and looked through them, out fell a postcard from Robert Frost!"

He didn't know who Robert Frost was, but obviously he was somebody his aunt liked a lot. "That's really something," he mumbled.

Aunt Cal picked up a handful of books and was back in the car before Trevor carried the boxes down. Maybe he should do ninety push-ups the next morning. By the time they got to Skyfield and unloaded the boxes and the groceries, he had revised the number. He'd try for ninety-five.

Aunt Cal was almost out of breath when she said, "If you don't mind one last chore, you could unpack the books, dust them off, and stack them on my desk. I'll look through them later. Now I must start cooking."

Unpacking the first box, Trevor wondered why anyone would want old books when they could go to the mall and buy new, clean ones. These smelled musty, like the pillow Other-Mother-Daphne brought down from the attic when he arrived for a visit.

They looked even more ancient than they smelled—yellowing arithmetics, ugly big geography books, history books that ended at World War I, and what must have been books for English classes—one book for each year up to eighth grade. People were lucky back then. At Meeker School he was supposed to read six whole books in one semester. Jessica had read five for him and had told him what happened so that he could write book reports.

The other box was no better. He made stacks of poetry, novels, and a story of some man's life written by himself before he died. Then came books for kids—animal books mostly. He had hated animal stories when he was a kid, especially the kinds where the animals thought and talked and lived in their own little houses with their own happy families.

He pulled out the last book, flicked his dust cloth

across the cover, and put it down on top of the pile. He glanced at it again. The girl on the jacket stared back at him. She looked like an old-fashioned Jessica, standing on a cliff with water behind her. *Steps on the Stairs: A Miranda York Mystery*, written by someone named Flavia LaRue. It sounded like an ice-cream flavor.

He was still thinking about Jessica after dinner when he went up to his room. The Scrabble players had set up their game on the sun porch and although no one had told him to get lost, that's what he always did when any of his parents had friends in. It was hard to ignore the shouts and moans and laughter from downstairs. He felt like the only kid who hadn't been invited to a birthday party.

He sat on his bed and wished he had someone to talk to or write to, but he'd sent a letter to his mother the day before and there was nothing new to tell her. He thought of the ad he'd read in Aunt Cal's magazine that morning. "Tired of friends who don't write? Eager for thoughtful communication?"

It took no time at all to run down to the mudroom, collect a bunch of last month's magazines, and get back to the bedroom. His mother had supplied him with enough stationery and stamps to last a year even if he wrote to every branch of his family tree.

Trevor began with "tired of friends who don't write," filled out the coupon, and addressed the envelope. Next, he sent for a booklet on how to stop smoking and a free catalog of exotic art. He almost skipped an ad that said "read books for pay," but decided it wouldn't be a bad deal if the books were short enough.

He sent for a sample recipe for Bulgarian moussaka and a brochure that included Amazon headdresses and morlock masks as well as details on "Esoteric Tours and Workshops of the Plumed Serpent." He was about to stop when he saw a small ad at the bottom of the page:

WANTED: Juvenile books from first half of century. Mint condition. Top prices. Interested in Ruth Fieldings, Elsie Dinsmores, Miranda York mysteries. Bookfinder, Box L, Grand Central Station, NY 10022

Miranda York mysteries? There was one on Aunt Cal's desk! Top price! He could sell the book for bus fare, and he wouldn't have to hock his Walkman. He wasn't sure what "mint condition" meant, but he'd be willing to negotiate. Real-Father negotiated often, so it must be legal.

He found a clean sheet of stationery and wrote as carefully as he could:

Dear Sir:

Please tell me how much you would pay for a Miranda York in mint condition.

At first, he thought of signing Trevor F. Ackerman, but changed his mind and wrote Freddie Ackerman, Skyfield, Blue Isle, Maine, as he had on all the other coupons.

He stacked the envelopes on the floor by his bed. In the morning he'd bike to the village before the post office opened and drop them in the outside pickup box. That way no one would wonder why he was writing so many letters.

It had grown dark outside, and the laughter from the sun porch was quieter. Maybe they were eating, or maybe they were sitting there talking with each other like friends. Talking reminded him of the ad about the twenty-four-hour-a-day philosopher.

He searched through four magazines before he found the 900 number, and just below it was Sister Linus. He wrote both numbers on a slip of paper and headed for the phone in Aunt Cal's library.

"Ten. Fourteen. Sixteen. Twenty-two and that's a double!" Lou shouted. "Our game!"

He shut the library door, glad he'd brought his flashlight so that he didn't have to turn on a lamp. Miranda York still lay on top of the stack of books. He picked it up. How could his aunt miss it if she'd never seen it? He dialed the first number and waited through beeps and dings and buzzes until a deep, full voice answered. It was the kind of voice that just by its rumble made Trevor feel good.

"Welcome, truth seeker. You have reached Stensrud the Philosopher, the interpreter of reason, logic, and the cognitive power of the human mind. Philosophy is the love of wisdom—*philo* for love and *sophy* for wisdom. Philosophy can explain the rationality, the reason for anything and everything, for it contains within itself all existence, beginning with Socrates and continuing through Locke and Kant. . . ."

"I called to ask you—" Trevor said, trying to interrupt, but Stensrud droned on as if he hadn't heard.

". . . and concerning the field of logic as opposed to psychology, either of which . . ."

"Listen!" Trevor tried again, "I called to ask if—"

The voice grew louder, as if every sentence ended in an exclamation point. "Philosophy is the study of man! It conceives the being of the world! It reveals the ultimate reality! It embodies the aesthetics and ideals of living!"

It was a recording. Trevor was listening to a tape!

He put the phone down on the desk and stood wondering how long the tape would run. He couldn't distinguish the words, but it didn't matter because they were only sounds strung together, meaning nothing. He finally hung up. He'd been ripped off! There was one more chance—Sister Linus.

Sister Linus was real!

He had to listen carefully because she spoke very slowly, just above a whisper, as if she were sharing a deep secret. She made him feel warm all over.

"And now, Freddie Ackerman, how can I help you?" she asked after he told her his name.

"I was wondering what you'd do if you had a whole bunch of parents and steppeople and a couple of great-aunts, and none of them really wanted you around."

"How old are you, Freddie?" The question went up and down like a caress.

He almost said fourteen, but she'd know the truth. "Twelve. I'll be thirteen at the end of the summer."

"And you're living with your parents?"

"No. Right now I'm with my great-aunts because Mom's in Bermuda with Charlie, but that's okay because she just married him. My original father lives in California and—" He stopped. "You know all that, don't you? You're psychic."

"Of course I know, Freddie," she whispered. "However, I need to listen to the texture of your voice."

He sat down on the desk chair. He'd never heard anyone say *however* out loud before, and he didn't know his voice had a texture.

She talked on about how hard it was, sometimes, to grow up. Trevor told her he'd been growing up all his life—that now he'd like to grow down, and she understood exactly what he meant.

She asked the day and month and year he was born, and after she consulted her chart and concentrated, she told him, "You have the innate wisdom to get yourself through anything that may trouble you. Have courage to do what you think best. Develop your concentrative powers as fully as you can so that you can bring your dreams down to earth and make them a reality. Dreams, you know, Freddie, can hide what's right in front of you. The moon is approaching your sign, Freddie, and everything is going to turn out beautifully for you."

He had no idea how long they talked, but finally Sister Linus said, "Now, Freddie, be *sure* and call back. I'll be thinking of you, studying your chart, and planning your future. Good-bye now."

The Scrabble players were still scrabbling as Trevor, Miranda York tucked under his arm, tiptoed up the stairs to his room. Sister Linus was thinking about *him*! She was studying his chart and planning his future! He stripped down to his shorts, climbed into bed—not bothering with pajamas—and pulled a pillow over his head so that he wouldn't lose the sound of Sister Linus's voice whispering secrets into his ear.

IT TOOK ONLY A WEEK before mail began to arrive for Freddie Ackerman. In the meantime, he'd had a couple of really important conversations with Sister Linus and he'd increased his pushups to ninety every morning.

Miss Florence frowned when Trevor and Lou walked into the post office, and kept on scowling as Lou unlocked the box and carried the big stack of mail over to the sorting counter. Lou picked up a skinny parcel wrapped in plain brown paper, looked at the address and then back at him. "*Freddie* Ackerman?" she asked.

"It's my middle name," he said loudly enough for Miss Florence to hear. "That's what they call me in Scouts. That's probably my Boy Scout magazine."

Evidently satisfied, the postmistress folded her arms

and leaned forward. "Did you hear about Stub Barnes, Louisa?" Not waiting for an answer, she added, "Claims he saw a storm petrel over on the beach at Smuggler's Cove."

"He did?" Lou stopped sorting mail and walked toward the cage. "Was it a Wilson?" She said *Wilson* as if it were some kind of password.

"He claimed it was." Miss Florence sounded as positive as Stub must have.

"I'd have to see it," Lou went on. "He thought he spotted one last year, but it wasn't. It was a Leach."

"I saw some Wilsons once when I was a child. Papa took me over to watch them come in to nest. They were all Wilsons then."

Lou shook her head. "They're a rare sight now, Wilsons are. Stub must have seen a Leach. You know how bad his eyes are."

The discussion of the nesting habits of petrels went on as Trevor hurriedly sorted the rest of the mail, rescuing one piece, marked "Confidential," from Pen Pals for Singles and a catalog of exotic art, only, when he opened the cover and looked inside, the word was *erotic*, not *exotic*. He must have misread the ad. By the time Lou came back to the counter, he had seven pieces of mail hidden away inside one of Aunt Cal's magazines.

Back at Skyfield, alone in his room, he spread his stash of mail on the bed. The brochure about lovely ladies of the world who wanted to make his acquaintance was nothing but pictures of young women in bikinis, along with lists of their vital statistics. Each one had a smile on her face, but none of them looked very happy.

The catalog of erotic art was mostly blurred photographs of the kinds of statues he'd seen when Miss Terkel took his class to the art museum. She'd rushed them past the rooms that held statues, but he and Jessica had sneaked back to one anyway. They couldn't figure out why Miss Terkel was so uptight—it was just a room full of stone people who looked cold without their clothes on.

It took Trevor a long time to go through the rest of his mail, especially the pictures in some of the other catalogs. He soon discovered that the ones wrapped in plain brown paper were the most interesting. When he opened the last envelope, he found five pages of patent information. He thought he'd sent for "Parent Information."

At dinner that evening, Lou asked, "Where were you all afternoon, Trevor? Out exploring again? Or catching up on your correspondence?"

He had a feeling she was laughing at him, so he looked down at his plate. "I was reading."

"That's nice, don't you think, Calla? We have another reader in the family."

Now he was sure she was laughing.

Aunt Cal smiled as she put a spoonful of fluffy whipped potatoes on his plate and passed it to him. He noticed that she sneaked a small helping for herself too while Lou was watching *him*. "What kinds of books interest you, Trevor? What are you reading?"

He knew a catalog of erotic art would be the wrong answer. He took a quick bite of the potatoes, as smooth as vanilla ice cream. The answer popped into his mind at the same time. He swallowed and looked up from his plate. "Flavia LaRue," he said.

There was complete silence.

"That's the name of the author. The book's about this kid—something York. I forget her first name." He looked at Aunt Cal's left eyebrow.

"Where did you find—?" That was Lou.

"You forgot her first name?" That was Aunt Cal.

Trevor put down his fork, then picked it up again. "I found it in one of those boxes we brought home. It's pretty beat-up and I figured you'd just throw it away." He looked from one to the other. "Have you ever heard of her? Flavia LaRue?"

"Never heard of her," both aunts said together. Aunt Cal went on, "What's the book about?"

Trevor tried very hard to remember what the cover of the book had looked like. "It's a mystery about this girl and it takes place in England during World War II, and she has to figure out who is sending signals to a German submarine. That's all I know so far."

"Fascinating," Lou murmured.

"Imaginative," Aunt Cal added. "You certainly may read the book, and if you enjoy it, perhaps there are others in the village library."

Trevor groaned silently. He'd made up a whole story for one book; he wasn't sure he had enough imagination to make up a whole summer full of plots—if his aunts kept him around that long.

"I'M GOING in after the mail," Lou called a few days later. "Do you want to come along?"

"I don't believe so," Trevor answered as he followed her down the back steps.

He sat on the steps and watched Lou back the station wagon out of the garage and chug out of the driveway, roaring along in low gear the entire length. He was so bored his brain wasn't working. Even the Walkman didn't help. The only station he could pick up played nothing but polkas and hymns.

There was nothing to look forward to on Blue Isle except the tides, the rain, and the mail. The tides were boring. The rain was boring. The mail was boring. How did you stop junk mail from coming? How was he supposed to know that the ads he'd answered didn't quit sending stuff? Instead the catalogs and brochures multiplied like some awful germ in a horror movie. The only solution was escape, as soon as he figured out the easiest way.

"Trevor," Aunt Cal called from inside, "could you come in for a minute?"

The model great-nephew he was still trying to be always answered yes to her questions.

"Yes," he answered.

"Could you carry these plants on the table over to the garage?"

The chores had begun shortly after his stacks of mail started arriving.

The plants were scraggly, ugly things that drooped over the edges of their pots and looked like stuff out of a technicolor nightmare. It took several trips before the table was cleared and the only thing left was a sick-looking tree almost bare of leaves.

He pressed his face against the screen door. "Do you want the big one in the corner to go, too?"

"Oh, not now. It's rather heavy. We'll wait with that one."

"What is it?"

"It *was* a lemon tree, Trevor," she said, and sighed. "Years ago we planted a lemon seed to see if it would grow. It did and we named it Lymon, but, as you can see, he's not doing too well at the moment. But there is Louisa. Would you help her take these books back to the library for me?"

"Yes," he answered. He couldn't understand why Lou needed help or why Aunt Cal took books from the library when she had a whole roomful of her own, but he took the stack that piled so high he had to use his chin to keep them balanced, and marched toward the station wagon.

"This is for Freddie," Lou said as he crawled in beside her. "Just one piece of mail today."

Sister Linus had used her psychic power! He'd told her about the flood of brown-paper wrappers and she'd known exactly what he felt. She always did. Trevor took the bulky envelope and tucked it under his seat.

"Do you have to answer all the mail you've been getting?" Lou asked as she turned the car around.

"Not really."

"Still, it's nice to have something to read, isn't it?" She was smiling as they drove away.

He expected to see a building with steps leading up to a big door with pillars and maybe a stone lion in front. Instead, they stopped in front of a little white house wrapped around by a wooden porch, stuck between a gift shop and a real estate office.

"This is it?" he asked.

"What matters is what's on the inside, not the outside." She took some of the books and walked toward the door.

It *had* been a regular house once. As soon as they were inside he could tell what had been a living room and a dining room right next to it. Now all the walls were lined with nothing but books.

Just inside the door, a woman sat behind a round oak table, her back to them. Lou put her books down and nodded for Trevor to do the same.

"The volume Miss Cal wanted came over from the mainland this morning. You can take it with you." The woman turned toward them. It was Smiley-Face Melva. "Young-adult books, Trevor, are beyond the kitchen." She pointed toward the back of the house. "In the laundry room."

He wasn't interested in books of any kind, but Lou had moved into the living room and was peering at the shelves, so he strolled in the direction Melva had gestured. He walked through the kitchen—full of encyclopedias, maps, and atlases—into the laundry room. He took one step inside and stopped. Crouched in a corner, leafing through a book, was Ariel, the lucky kid who didn't have a father.

"Hi, Trevor." She sounded as if they'd known each other forever.

"What are you doing here?" She looked like something someone had forgotten to remember to pick up.

"Looking for a book I haven't read."

Trevor glanced at the shelves of books that reached the ceiling. "You've read them all?"

"All the good ones." She stood up, put a book back on the shelf, and pulled out another. "I like stories about kids who have problems, don't you? I can always figure out what they should do before they think of it."

"I don't read. I mean, I don't read books like that."

"What do you read then?"

He wished she'd quit asking him about books. He had to read them in school. Wasn't that enough? He leaned against the doorway and lied in what Jessica called his lava-acid voice. "I like factual books—adult books. I really prefer TV because it takes too long for things to happen when you're reading. On TV, it can all be over with in half an hour. Don't you have a television set?"

"I do when I live with my mom. It's a huge one that

fills up most of one wall. Reading's more fun, though, because you can do it anywhere."

"Are you taking all those?" He couldn't believe it. She picked up a stack of books almost as high as Aunt Cal's and started toward the door.

"Melva lets me take out seven at a time. One for each day of the week."

"You read one a day?" He stepped aside to let her pass. He wished she wouldn't leave.

"Sometimes two," she answered as she hurried through the kitchen.

He hoped she'd say, "Why don't you bike over and see me sometime?" She didn't.

On the drive back to Skyfield, they passed her, pedaling a bike that looked even older than the Schwinn. She didn't wave or even look up as they went by.

Girls were hard to figure out. One minute they acted as if they liked you and the next they pretended they didn't even know you. That was the trouble with being twelve. Maybe it would be different next year.

HE WAS HALFWAY up the stairs to get rid of his latest piece of mail when he heard Aunt Cal shout from the library, "Louisa, whom have we been calling in California?"

Trevor stopped in midstep.

"We haven't called anyone," Lou answered from down the hall.

Trevor peeked over the banister. Aunt Cal bustled out of the library, paging through a sheaf of bills. "Well, look at this, will you. A call to San Francisco for ten minutes!"

How could he have forgotten? Those 900 numbers weren't toll-free. Could he possibly have listened to Stensrud's tape for ten minutes? It hadn't seemed that long.

"This is an outrage, Louisa. The phone company has made an error. I'll report it right now."

Lou joined her and examined the bills. "Do you suppose Trevor has been calling his father after we were in bed? Look at the time of the calls."

Trevor held his breath. Where could he hide? Aunt Cal hadn't come to Sister Linus yet.

"Good Heavenly Graces!" That was Aunt Cal.

"His father lives in Dana Point, though." That was Lou.

"Here's one to Los Angeles." The pages crackled.

"One?" echoed Lou. "Two! Three! Four!"

Aunt Cal picked up the count. "Five! Six! I'm going to call the telephone company. There's some terrible mistake." She started toward the library.

"Wait, Calla." Lou grabbed her arm. "I think we have a dilemma here."

"A dilemma?" Aunt Cal was close to shouting.

"A twelve-year-old dilemma. Outside of you and me and Melva, who's never here at night, there's only one person who could have made these calls."

"Trevor." Aunt Cal spoke more softly, almost whispering his name.

Lou went on. "I have an inkling there's a connection between the quantity of his mail and these bills. Let's just pay them and call it a learning experience."

Trevor waited to hear an answer, but the library door slammed shut. He'd really done it this time! He'd start packing his bags, but he didn't want to be cornered in the bedroom trying to explain Sister Linus. He started back down the stairs and came face to face with Lou.

"I assume you heard," she said smiling.

He tried to say yes, but settled for a nod. Lou's smile could be hazardous.

"You owe your Aunt Calla one-hundred and three dollars and fifty-six cents." She was still smiling, but her voice wasn't. "That is about how much it would be worth for you to weed the flower beds around the house and garage, and when you're through with that, to prune the raspberry patch."

"When do I start?"

Freddie Ackerman, prisoner, knew when he didn't have a chance. The evidence was indisputable. He felt the cold steel enclose his ankles and the heavy drag of the chain as he was herded out to labor in the lime quarry.

"How about now," Lou said.

THAT NEXT WEEK it became evident that his aunts loved flowers—flowers of all kinds, which he'd never noticed before. Even the raspberry brambles beyond the garage were a welcome relief from crawling around on his hands and knees weeding petunias, salvia, roses, and geraniums—red geraniums that made his nose drip.

As he labored through the week, mail for Freddie Ackerman tapered off so that finally there wasn't one single catalog or pamphlet or one of those personal letters with his computerized name at the beginning and friendly little *Freddie's* tucked in after every other sentence.

Then, the very next day, as he sat on the steps resting from raspberries, Lou dropped a letter into his lap. "Freddie Ackerman strikes again," she chirped.

He was beginning to hate the name.

This envelope was not like the others he'd received. The address was handwritten. He waited until Lou left before he tore it open.

Dear Freddie Ackerman,

I am most interested in your copy of the Miranda York mystery *Steps on the Stairs*.

It was an answer from the Bookfinder!

I would like, however, to verify if the book which you possess is the particular edition my client is seeking.

Would you please check to see 1) if there is such a place as Smuggler's Cove on Isle d'Bas and if the description in the text matches the actual locale, and

2) if the Isle really does contain burial sites of ancient people.

If you will provide me with this information, I'll be happy to negotiate a price, ranging from $50 to, perhaps, $500.

Five hundred dollars! Tens and twenties were easy to imagine, but hundreds? With five hundred, he could escape Blue Isle. He could go anywhere—maybe to Colorado and camp up in the mountains for the rest of the summer.

All he had to do was read a few pages, find a description, and figure out how to get to Isle d'Bas, wherever that was. Ariel! She had said something about her grandfather's mail boat. Maybe he went there. Trevor would ask for a ride. He'd even offer to pay.

First, the book! He ran to his room, pulled Miranda York out from under his socks, sprawled out on the bed, and began to read:

Miranda York leaned up against the boulder and stared down at the waves rolling in crests and trenches toward shore and shattering into spray against jagged rocks below. A gray mist of rain drizzled through larches, sifting soundlessly to the needle-strewn ground. Suddenly Miranda noticed a dark figure creeping among the rocks below. It paused, looked around, pulled out a flashlight, and blinked it on and off, three times.

Puzzled, Miranda peered through the drizzle, only to see an answering flash far out in the harbor.

It wasn't bad. He read on as Miranda, whose mother just happened to be a ham-radio operator, so she knew shortwave codes, easily made out the cryptic message: "Smuggler's Cove."

"Trevor! Are you there?" Aunt Cal called up the stairs. "There's some real lunch for a change."

"I'm not hungry," he answered. He couldn't leave Miranda yet.

"You're not sick, are you?"

"No. I just need to finish doing something. I mean reading something."

He looked down at the book. He was on page 30. When he got to the description of the cove, he reread it several times until he practically had it memorized. Then he decided it would be a good idea to copy the whole thing.

After that it would be time to find Ariel.

THE AFTERNOON WAS PERFECT for bicycling, with hardly any breeze, the air still cool from an early dawn shower, and the sun deliciously warm on his back. Aunt Cal's bicycle didn't begin to compare with his own ten-speed Trek at home, but with the Schwinn's big balloon tires, it was perfect for jumping off the road and flying down into the ditch and out again like a professional road-bike racer.

He could almost feel his leg muscles developing as he pedaled full speed out toward the causeway. He was positive that along with his morning calisthenics he might be big enough to go out for soccer next fall. Jessica said football was a no-brain activity, but that soccer took not only muscle, but speed and brains. He hadn't had room to pack his soccer ball. He had brought his Hacky-Sack, though, but a Hacky-Sack wasn't much fun if there was no one around to watch.

The tide was out when he reached the causeway, and instead of water lapping against the roadside, there were long stretches of mud flats. Like the day he first came to Blue Isle, clammers were out with their pails, wading around, up to their knees in muck. He parked the Schwinn and sat down beside the road to watch and rest. That was one thing he could say about Blue Isle: There was always time to sit and watch . . . and think, if he wanted to, or not think if he didn't want to. He'd left his Walkman back in his room. He had something worth thinking about now: five hundred dollars!

One clammer was out almost to the edge of the receding tide, while a kid stood back with a pail. The man tossed something and the kid fielded it like a baseball throw. Their laughter echoed across the flats. The man turned, looked toward shore, and pointed at Trevor. The kid turned.

"Hi, Trevor."

It wasn't just any kid. It was Ariel! How lucky could he get?

"Come on out and help. It's fun. Take off your shoes."

Trevor looked down at his sky-blue shorts and the new tank top his mother had sent him from Bermuda. He was about to refuse, but he thought about the five hundred dollars and the book and the chance to catch a ride out to Isle d'Bas, and he tugged off his sneakers and slogged out toward the clammers.

"What do I do?" Cold, slimy mud oozed between his toes.

Ariel picked up a pail and moved farther out toward the tide line. "I'll rake. You pick," she called back. "But you'll have to come out farther than that."

He'd never waded in mud that deep before. It was fun, really, pulling one leg and then the other out of the slipperiness with a slurp that sounded as if he were being sucked back in. Maybe that was what quicksand felt like. He'd seen something like that on TV once, where a murderer got caught in a swamp full of hidden pits of quicksand that sucked him clear under.

He peered into the pail Ariel was holding. He'd never seen live clams before. They could have been any old rocks as they lay covering the bottom of the pail. Ariel picked up a five-pronged rake and moved ahead.

"How do you know where they are?"

"Easy," she answered. "Look! There's one. When they're disturbed, they spurt out water. That's when you have to rake fast because they'll try to dig down deeper. While I rake, you grab. See?"

By the time their pail was half full, Trevor was muddy up to his elbows, and his blue shorts were a spattered gray. He soon learned how to locate the clams with his toes. As he and Ariel were bent over, she raking and he catching them, a deep voice said, "Trevor's a pretty good helper, I see." The man, his trousers rolled up above his knees, looked down into their pail. "I think you two snagged more than I did." He could have been the sheriff on "Son of a Gun," rugged and leathery like on TV.

"How'd you know my name?"

"This is my grandpa. He knows all about you," Ariel said. "I told him. You can call him Captain."

"You're pretty good for an off-islander."

He wasn't just saying it either, Trevor could tell, because their pail did hold a lot more clams than his.

"I think it's time to quit. Throw your bicycle in the back of the truck, Trevor. We'll go home and get cleaned up. Climb in the back with Ariel."

By the time they reached the mobile home, the sun and hot wind had dried and caked their arms and legs into what felt like giant mud packs. The Captain picked up the pails of clams and started for the lean-to. "The two of you better get under the hose and wash off some of that real estate."

After the hosing, Trevor and Ariel sat in the sun on two rusty lawn chairs and dried off during a lunch of potato chips and Snickers candy bars. It wasn't until then that he remembered why he'd come looking for her. How could he have forgotten? How, though, did he go about asking her if he could get a ride on her grandpa's boat? At first he thought of telling her about the book and the money he was going to make, but he wasn't sure he wanted to share all that.

"Didn't you tell me once," he began as he crumpled

the wrapper from his second Snickers, "that your grandpa runs the mail boat?"

"Sure."

"And that he carries mail out to the other islands?"

"Yes. Why?"

"My aunts were talking about some place I ought to see. Smuggler's Cove?"

"Sure, that's on Isle d'Bas. He stops there."

"Well," he began, nonchalantly he hoped, "do you suppose he'd let me ride along some morning? I'll pay."

"Sure he would. If I asked him, but you won't have to pay. I still have your three dollars. When do you want to go?"

It was that easy! "Whenever he'll let me." He tried not to appear too eager.

"I'll go ask him now." She scrambled up and ran back into the mobile home.

Trevor lay back in his chair, his hands behind his head, and decided that instead of spending the five hundred dollars to get off Blue Isle, he'd save it all and when he got home he'd buy a hot-pink Yamaha Razz moped. That would make Jessica talk to him again.

"He said to be down at the end of your drive by four tomorrow morning," Ariel shouted as she came running back. "We'll pick you up . . . if it's all right with your aunts."

"You going too?"

"If you're going. It'll be fun."

"Do you know where Smuggler's Cove is?"

"Everybody does. I'll show you."

Trevor didn't realize how early four o'clock in the morning was, nor how much quieter Blue Isle could be at that hour. Only a single faint chirp from deep among the pines broke the stillness of the predawn as he jogged down the drive. Aunt Cal had thought the trip on the mail boat with Ariel and her grandfather a "capital idea" and had even helped him set his alarm and hunted up an extra sweatshirt for him. Maybe she was glad to get rid of him. He didn't have long to wait before he heard the distant hum of the pickup.

"Fair skies and calm seas," the Captain announced as Trevor climbed into the cab beside Ariel. "Promises a perfect trip. But you two aren't making the entire run, are you?"

"No," Ariel answered for Trevor. "He wants to see Smuggler's Cove."

"That's fine. It's our first stop. No smugglers left, though."

Trevor felt in his back pocket. It was still there—the description of the cove he'd copied from the Flavia LaRue mystery. He might have to read it over again in order to verify every detail for the Bookfinder.

The Stoneport harbor was full of tired-looking fishing smacks, dingy gray against the black water, docks cluttered with empty lobster pots, coils of rope, and nets drying in the predawn breeze. Everything smelled of fish and saltwater and tar.

"You two get on board while I pick up the mail pouches." Ariel's grandfather nodded toward the dock.

Trevor followed Ariel down the length of the pier and into the boat. A faint line of pale light was beginning to form on the eastern horizon. He couldn't remember when he'd ever been up early enough to see the sunrise. He knew he had never seen a sunrise over an ocean.

The Captain soon returned, toting several mail pouches, and with a few coughs and sputters and whines from the motor, they were under way. Trevor stood alone in the stern. Ariel disappeared into the cabin with her grandfather as the old boat's motor, sounding like an overloaded, off-balance washing machine on hard spin, churned out a foamy wake. Once outside the harbor, the water became choppy in spite of the Captain's assurance of calm seas. Trevor was glad he hadn't eaten breakfast as Aunt Cal had suggested.

He liked the feel of the wind blowing through his hair as the Stoneport harbor melted into the morning mist. There was no need to pretend. He really *was* Freddie Ackerman, going out to verify a location, with the almost certain possibility of receiving a handsome reward for his trouble. It was not too long before a tiny spot of green loomed up before them.

"Isle d'Bas," the Captain announced as he shut down the motor to a soft hum. He dropped the two of them off on the island with a small bag of letters and parcels, then headed back out into the bay, gulls following in his wake like dive-bombers. Ariel picked up the mailbag and headed for a building that could have been a store or a post office or a bait shop or all three.

"Where's everybody?" Trevor asked, following her up the wooden steps leading from the pier.

"In the first place, it's only five in the morning. In the second place, there isn't such a thing as everybody around here, only a few somebodies. Summer people, mostly, along with Joe Bates, who lives here year round."

She set the mailbag down in front of the all-purpose store, slipped off a key that hung from a string around her neck, unlocked what looked like an old sea chest, and dropped the mailbag inside.

"Do you do this every morning?" The sun still hadn't come up, and he was sure the two of them were the only ones awake on the island.

"Just on Tuesdays and Thursdays. Sometimes I stay here and wait for Joe to open his store. Then I wait inside until Grandpa picks me up on the way back. Smuggler's Cove is this way." She started up a path that disappeared among trees.

"Aren't there any roads?"

"Why roads? There aren't any cars. Everybody rides a bicycle or walks. Except for Joe Bates. He has a couple of horses over on the other side of the island."

It was dark and silent as they followed a path through pines like poles topped with thatches of green and around rocks as large as houses. Finally they climbed up onto a gray rock that loomed above a rocky cove. The ocean beyond was dappled with sunlight.

"It's like a picture," Trevor said, not sure if what he was seeing was real or if he was just imagining it was real because of the handwritten description tucked in his back pocket. "Who owns all this?"

"It's a preserve."

"What are they preserving?"

Ariel grabbed his arm and pointed across to the sandy beach far below. "Don't move! They're back!"

"Who's back?" He looked around, moving nothing but his eyeballs, half expecting to see a boatload of Miranda York's smugglers emerging from the ocean mist.

"Petrels! And they're nesting!"

He saw them then, flocks of birds, fluttering and dipping toward shore. "Don't all birds nest?"

"They haven't nested *here* for years." She talked so low she might as well have been telling him a long-hidden secret.

"Where have they been?"

"No one really knows. I think maybe people crowded them out. See, what they do is dig burrows in the sand for their eggs. Then the males sit on the eggs during the day while the females go out over the ocean for food. At dawn they change places. That's what they're doing now. Changing places."

It was like a movie he had watched on Jessica's VCR one night, where all these birds came out and got into people's hair and pecked their way into houses. What seemed like hundreds of birds kept flying in from the ocean, cooing and squeaking and gurgling as they greeted each other, going and coming from nest to sea and sea to nest. Ariel still held his arm, and with the early morning sky dark with birds, he hoped she wouldn't let go.

"Grandpa says petrels are the souls of drowned sailors. They bring good luck, though. That's why no sailor would ever kill one."

Trevor had always thought petrel was what the British put in their gas tanks. "You'd think they'd bump into each other. Or get in the wrong nest."

"They're not like other birds. They can see in the dark. Nobody'll believe us, but I *know* they're Wilsons."

With the quiet mutter of ocean against rock, the strange cooing, chuckling calls of the Wilsons, the sky caught between night and dawn, Trevor felt as if he were trapped in some kind of spell. The sun touched Ariel's hair, turning it a sandy gold, and for a moment she looked almost pretty. "Wow!" was all he could say, but it didn't begin to express what he felt.

"Let's not disturb them." Ariel climbed down off the rock. "Come on. There's something else I want to show you." She started back the way they'd come, turned, and disappeared behind a boulder the size of a compact car. A faint path among the trees led to a jumble of rocks that looked as if some primitive giant had pitched them up on shore. Ariel was standing under three heavy stones arranged to form a crude doorway, with two stones set upright and the third extended across the top. "Red Paint People buried their dead in places marked like this. There are two others farther on."

He couldn't believe his luck! It was exactly what he'd read in the Miranda York mystery. Did the government make a five-hundred-dollar bill, or would the Bookfinder send five separate one-hundred-dollar bills?

"What are Red Paint People?" Flavia LaRue hadn't explained that.

"Ancient skeletons buried in red soil. No one knows where the red soil came from so they called them Red Paint People. I read a book that said they came across the ocean thousands of years ago and fished and hunted here. But we'd better start back now."

She led him zigzagging through trees and brush on a path that only she could see. Just when Trevor thought she was lost, the trees opened up and they were standing beside a weathered-gray house perched on the very edge of a cliff.

"This way," Ariel shouted as she led him around the house to a redwood deck that overlooked the harbor where the Captain had dropped them off. Ariel unfolded a couple of lawn chairs and motioned Trevor to sit.

"What about the people who live here?" Trevor glanced around, expecting someone to open the front door and order them off the premises.

"Tansy doesn't open her house until the summer people leave." Ariel moved her chair closer to the edge. "I like it here. It's a good place to come when I'm lonesome."

"For your mom?"

"For *me*. Sometimes I have to be really alone to remember who I am."

Gulls circled over the water below. A loon dived deep and reappeared with a momentary flash of silver in its beak, and farther up the beach, dainty sandpipers minced along the sand.

"It's illegal, isn't it? When it isn't ours?"

Ariel sat back, closed her eyes, and propped her feet up on the ledge. "We're here now and she isn't. Besides, she wouldn't care, so it belongs to us."

"That's only pretending."

"So what?" She opened her eyes. "It's only a problem if you can't tell the difference between what's real and what's pretending. See, there's the person I want to be and the person I pretend to be and the person I really am. Sometimes it's hard to tell who you are, don't you think?"

It was something he'd felt, but he'd never told anyone! "Do you ever get it all together?"

Ariel yawned and wiggled back into her chair. "I don't think anyone does. Grandpa says grown-ups are just big kids with bank accounts and credit cards."

Trevor laughed and settled back in his chair, feeling as if he owned the big house behind him and all the land and water as far as he could see.

Ariel went on to explain how Tansy had been coming to the house from the time she was a child, how she and her husband brought their own children there each summer, and how Tansy had now outlived them all, even her own children, but she still came back to the island every autumn.

"Tansy says the house is her family now," Ariel concluded.

He wondered what house he'd pick to visit when he was old: Mom's last apartment? The new condo? Other-Father-Norman's duplex? Real-Father's ranch house? Skyfield?

"Families aren't houses! They're people you have to live with whether you want to or not." He'd never said that to anyone before either.

Ariel went on as if she hadn't heard him. "One person who loves you is enough to make a family . . . even if that person isn't around anymore."

It didn't make sense. Trevor did what he always did when someone was telling him something he didn't want to believe—he quit thinking.

Ariel sat up. "I brought some sandwiches. Peanut butter and jelly. Want one?"

Trevor hated peanut-butter-and-jelly sandwiches. Jessica said they were really goober grease and mouthwash, but sitting looking out from Tansy's cliff house with the sun blazing across the harbor, he had to admit he'd never eaten anything that tasted so good.

By the time Ariel and her grandfather dropped him off at Skyfield's drive, the morning was gone. He'd have to hurry to get his letter written to the Bookfinder and pedal down to the village before the late-afternoon mail went out.

It took him longer than he'd figured to write the letter. He wrote more than he'd intended, but he thought he had to tell about his trip on the mail boat and the petrels and the burial sites and Tansy's home on the cliff . . . and he had to copy over one part because he'd made a mistake. He came out of the post office after mailing the letter, still practically breathless from pedaling the Schwinn at top speed all the way there, when he saw Ariel astraddle her bike out by the curb.

"You forgot your sweatshirt. What are you doing?"

"Mailing a letter."

"Do you answer all the mail you get?"

Trevor walked over to his bike. "How do you know how much mail I get?"

"I heard Florence tell Aunt Melva that you got more mail than anyone else on the island. Anyway, here's your sweatshirt. If you're going back to Skyfield, I'll ride along."

What could he say? He couldn't think of anything else to do, and she was a whole lot better than nothing.

He started up the hill leading out of the village and, cresting the top, he let go the handlebars, folded his arms across his chest, and coasted down. As he grabbed the handlebars again, Ariel glided up beside him, her arms folded across her chest, flashing a triumphant grin. Not saying a word, Trevor cut a number three in the sand along the stretch of level road. Ariel followed with a perfect eight of her own.

"Do you have to do everything I do?" It wasn't that she did it. It was that she did it better.

"It's a free country, isn't it?"

"I suppose. But if you can't think of something original . . ."

It was the way she looked at him, her lips pressed together, that made him decide not to bug her anymore. They rode in silence, side by side, until they reached the drive leading to Skyfield.

"Race you up to Aunt Cal's garage." It sounded like a dare, but he hoped she understood it was an invitation.

"You're on!" she agreed.

She won.

"You ever been over there on the little island?" He pointed to the cove.

"No."

"Want to go?"

"Why not?"

He started across the rocks. She sat down, took off her sneakers, and followed, moving from rock to rock like a ballet dancer.

"This island's mine," he said. "I mean, I call it mine. I named it Lost Island."

She sat down, her back to the big tree. He walked over and sat down beside her.

"Do your aunts care if we're out here?" She leaned back against the tree trunk.

"Why should they? Just so we go back before the tide comes in." He hoped his aunts hadn't told anyone about Homer's rescuing him that day. Secrets like that should be kept. He had secrets he kept from even himself.

Ariel stretched out on the grass, cushioning her head on one arm. "Exciting, isn't it? To think we're sitting right on top of their graves."

"Whose graves?"

"You know. The two lovers. Haven't you heard about them?"

"I don't believe that stuff."

She looked different, somehow, lying on the grass beside him.

"They loved each other so much they'd rather die in each other's arms than live apart."

Water splashed against the rocks, and if he didn't know better, he could think the island was slowly drifting out into the bay. Ariel was so close that all he'd have to do was barely move his arm and he could touch her.

Jessica told him she'd kissed Greg McMann once, right on the mouth! She said her life had never been the same since. He wondered if it worked for boys. Ariel tilted her head to one side. Why had Jessica said *she* kissed Greg? Why didn't she say *Greg* kissed her? Didn't boys kiss girls sometimes?

He moved his arm. His hand rested no more than a couple of inches from Ariel's shoulder. Her eyes were closed. He leaned closer and wished he'd paid attention to what they did next on those afternoon soaps on TV.

Maybe he should say something first. Whisper something, maybe, but what? Maybe he should ask her if he could. One thing he knew. *His* life could stand a change!

Just when he was about to move even closer, Ariel opened her eyes. With one leap she stood up and rushed toward him, giving him a push that rocked him back and sent him sprawling, arms outstretched.

"I don't do suck-face, Trevor Ackerman!" she shouted, and before he could sit up, she ran across the rocks and disappeared.

He didn't follow to try to explain. There was nothing he could say. Jessica was right, as usual. Boys didn't kiss girls. Girls kissed boys. Maybe when he was thirteen, it'd be different.

ARIEL WAS NOWHERE AROUND the next day, and Trevor convinced himself that he was glad as he sat on the steps and turned up the volume on his Walkman. He was giving up on girls forever—at least until he was a year older.

He liked the way the music filled his ears, matching his heartbeat and setting his whole body alive and moving with the rhythm. He could sit and look and not even see. He could listen and not think. He could forget without remembering what he was trying to forget.

A tap on his shoulder interrupted the music, and he turned down the volume. Lou was standing behind him.

"I asked if you're busy. Are you?"

"Not very." He pulled off the earphones and hung

them around his neck. "I think my batteries are running out again anyway."

"If you can untangle yourself from that thing, I could use a little help."

"Now?"

"Now. Everything *but* now was a long time ago." She stood slightly bent forward, as if she were running ahead of herself.

"What are you going to do?"

"We are going to take a load of your aunt's discards to the Second-Time-Around Bookstore. They've been stacked in there"—she nodded toward the mudroom— "since last Christmas. She's finally decided she can part with them. I'll get the wagon and you can help me put them in the back."

He propped open the screen door and carried out the first box. The push-ups must have worked. Even if his arms didn't look bigger, the box was lighter than the one he'd carried a few weeks before. By the time Lou backed up to the steps and opened the tailgate, he had all six boxes stacked up outside and he wasn't even breathing hard.

"Want me to come along and help unload? Maybe we could stop in the village and I could get some new batteries."

"Try to be quiet," she whispered as loudly as a whisper could get. "We don't want Calla to hear us."

"I thought you said she wanted us to take them away.

We're not stealing them, are we?" He thought of Miranda York hidden under his bed.

"Of course we aren't stealing anything. Your aunt is a pack rat and always has been—especially when it comes to books. If she knows we actually *are* taking them this morning, she'll find a reason to keep them even if she doesn't want them."

"They aren't worth anything, are they? There's nothing she could sell?"

Lou shook her head. "Totally worthless in terms of time and space."

"But what if . . ." Trevor tried to put into words an uncomfortable half-idea that bothered him. "What if inside one of the books there was a fifty-dollar bill and somebody at the bookstore found it? Who would it belong to?"

"Whom would it belong to?" she repeated, stressing the *m*. "It would be a matter of ethics, I suppose. A person could give it back to your aunt. Then Calla would have to decide whether to keep it or give it back to the original owner of the book. Why? Do you think we should empty the cartons and start shaking books?"

"No." Her answer hadn't helped. He reached out to close the tailgate.

Lou stopped him. "This is a perfect time to do away with Lymon. He's been dead since *before* Christmas, but Calla won't bury him."

He knew she was talking about the withered tree, but

117

for a minute she sounded like the murderer he'd seen on "Mystery!"

She was already headed toward the wasted, brittle lemon tree that listed in the corner of the mudroom. "We've tried everything short of mouth-to-mouth resuscitation, and nothing works."

Her words were somehow familiar.

"Calla once thought he'd straighten up with support. In an off moment, I suggested we talk to him even if he is as dead as last week's fish." She marched toward Lymon.

Her words were *more* than familiar! Trevor had heard them floating up through the hot-air register one of those first rainy mornings. His aunts hadn't been talking about him. They'd been discussing a stupid tree!

He felt light-headed, and leaned against the door. How could he have been so dumb? How could he have been so wrong? Maybe they weren't delighted to have Trevor around for the summer, but it was Lymon they wanted to get rid of.

"I'll do it," Trevor offered. He knelt down, wrapped his arms around the plastic pot, and, tottering under its weight, carried it through the door Lou held open, and stowed dead Lymon in the wagon. "He's going to the dump, isn't he?"

"You've read my mind," Lou said. "Best place I can think of to get rid of a mistake, and a lemon tree in Maine is a big mistake."

The road that led to the village dump wasn't really a

road—it was even narrower and bumpier than the drive into Skyfield. It didn't seem to bother Lou as she clutched the steering wheel with both hands and pointed the wagon down the middle of the ruts.

"I'll take care of it," Trevor said before Lou stopped. He'd never be able to tell her how good it felt to tug the dried-up tree out of the back and heave it down into the landfill, where it came to rest next to someone's discarded barbecue grill.

"It's a tough life, Lymon," he whispered, "but you can't raise lemons in Maine."

The road out was even narrower than the road in. Trevor hoped it was one-way. He would have asked, except he didn't want Lou to stop concentrating on her driving. They were almost back to the main road—he could see it through the trees—when some invisible force started pulling his side of the wagon toward the soggy shallow ditch. He leaned forward in his nonexistent seat belt and grabbed the armrest.

"Hang on," Lou grunted, and floored the gas pedal. The station wagon grunted too, and groaned and shuddered, its tires spinning. Then, with a lurch and a splatter of mud that covered Trevor's window, they were headed straight again.

"Are you okay?" he asked as soon as he started breathing once more.

"Certainly," Lou answered. "I could drive this with my eyes closed."

He was beginning to think that was how she did drive, but he didn't say so.

When they reached the bookstore, Trevor carried the boxes around to the back and piled them in a corner, while Lou complained to one of Melva's cousins, who owned the place. "You'd think the village could maintain that stretch as well as any other road on the island."

Finally, when they got to the post office, Lou went in for the mail, and Trevor scooted down to Will's Groceries for the Walkman batteries. He'd just finished installing them when his aunt climbed into the car beside him.

"Florence asked if anything's wrong. Seems there wasn't any mail for you today." Lou slammed the door and started the engine.

Commander Freddie Ackerman gritted his teeth and cursed the informer who posed as a postmistress. It was because of her that he was handcuffed and nearly helpless. Despite the captor beside him, he strained to use the radio hidden in his clothing. He must make contact with his men in the submarine that lurked deep in the waters of the bay.

Brakes screeching, the station wagon came to an abrupt halt, jolting the earphones off Trevor's head. A state-police car, its lights blinking, stood at the side of the road, and a trooper walked toward them.

"Just a routine check," he said, smiling. "Would you turn on your headlights, please? Bright first, then dim."

It wasn't Homer. It was a stranger from the mainland

120

who moved to the front of the wagon. "Now your turning signals," he called. "I'll check them from the back, too. And then just step on the brake for a minute, if you would."

Lou was breathing as if she'd been running instead of driving.

"That's fine, ma'am. Everything's working fine." The trooper was bent almost in half as he leaned down to talk through Lou's window. "Now, I need to look at your driver's license."

Lou muttered something Trevor couldn't understand and began shuffling through her billfold. It took awhile, but finally she thrust the plastic card out the window and muttered again.

"What did you say?" Trevor whispered.

"I said 'rats,' " she whispered back.

"Well now, ma'am," the trooper squatted down so that his eyes were level with Lou's. "I'm afraid this license has expired."

"I can't imagine how that happened." Lou's voice sounded so sweet that Trevor blinked.

"It's about two years expired," the officer went on.

"How could I have overlooked that?" She didn't sound like the aunt Trevor knew.

"You're not restricted to glasses, I see."

"Of course not." She turned toward the trooper with a triumphant smile.

"I don't want to give you a ticket, but I will give you a warning." He pulled a pad of paper from his pocket and began writing. "You have ten days to get this license renewed, and then everything will be in order. Do you have someone to drive for you?"

"Not this car."

Trevor looked over at his aunt and then quickly glanced in the opposite direction.

"I'll give you a waiver good for ten days. Just sign here." He finished scribbling, tore off the sheet, and handed it to Lou to sign. When she returned it, he touched his cap in a kind of salute and signaled them to drive on.

"What a lovely man," Lou said as she stepped on the gas. "I appreciate respect for niceties."

"You said there was no one to drive for you." What he meant was that she'd lied.

"You weren't listening, Trevor," she answered, eyes glued to the road. "I said I had no one to drive *this* car. There is a difference." She was quiet the rest of the way back to Skyfield, and then she spoke again without looking at him. "I don't think we should bother Calla with that nonsense back there, do you?"

"Are you sure?" he asked.

"Trust me. Trust me. There's always a chance that I might be right. Anyway, an important letter just came for her, and we mustn't worry her about unimportant things like licenses."

Trevor didn't have a chance to consider ratting on Lou because the letter sent Aunt Cal into a surge of action even before she finished reading it for the second time. He hadn't known that she could move so quickly.

122

In the midst of striding through the house, she announced, "I must go into the city. That's New York City, Trevor."

Maybe she felt as trapped on Blue Isle as he did. The difference was that she must know somebody who wanted to see her and even sent a letter inviting her.

"I'll leave tomorrow, Louisa, if you'll call and confirm the reservation. The tickets have already been paid for." She waved the letter. "What shall I wear?"

Trevor thought about suggesting her purple caftan. That way no one would have trouble finding her when she got off the plane.

"Why not your purple caftan?" Lou said the words for him. "And, Calla, would you have time to get me some of those milk chocolates from the shop on Fifth? Do you suppose you'll be anywhere near the Garden Shop? You might pick up one of those Accelerated Propagation Systems—the trays for seedlings with domes over them."

It took the rest of the day and most of the next morning for his aunts to get everything organized. Lou made lists and schedules and confirmed the plane tickets and hotel reservations. Aunt Cal made mysterious notes to herself, then packed and repacked two very large suitcases. Trevor decided this was the most exciting thing that had happened to any of them since he was stranded on Lost Island.

"Are you sure, Trevor, that you don't want to come to Bangor with us?" Aunt Cal asked in the morning. "You really don't mind staying here alone tonight?" She stood in the middle of the kitchen, staring at her luggage stacked by the doorway.

He tried to look as if he were seriously considering his answer. Jessica said if you took a few seconds to say something, people would think you were thinking. "I'll be fine. I'll find a book to read." The lie was easy. "I'll go to bed early. Besides, what could happen? This is Blue Isle."

She started to leave, then hesitated. "You know the plane doesn't depart until six, and Louisa could certainly drive back. I would feel better, though, if she stays over with our friends and comes home in the morning."

"I understand," Trevor said. "I really do." Maybe he'd try calling Ariel. It couldn't be long distance, and she must have a phone.

"The names and numbers of our friends are on the desk in the library."

He knew her words by heart. She'd repeated them at least ten times in the last two hours.

"All right, then, if you're sure," Aunt Cal went on. "Louisa will probably be back here in the morning before you wake up, if I know her." She looked at her luggage again. "I wonder if I should pack just one more pair of . . ." Her words trailed off as she hoisted a suitcase and headed toward the stairs.

By late that day and after two more suitcase shuffles, Aunt Cal and her luggage were settled in the station wagon, Lou was behind the wheel, and Trevor was saying good-bye for the third time.

"Now don't forget," Aunt Cal said. "Dinner is in the refrigerator and Louisa's telephone number is—"

"On your desk in the library," he finished for her. "Don't worry about me."

He was moving back toward the house when Lou called to him. "Trevor, I almost forgot to give you Freddie Ackerman's mail. Here, Calla, hand it to him."

As the wagon pulled away, Trevor waved once and grinned. The house was empty and he'd sit at the kitchen table and look through his correspondence. Maybe by this time, Jessica had changed her mind and written to him.

The junk mail hadn't stopped after all. He found a catalog of kitchen equipment, a sample box of dishwashing detergent, and two pamphlets from a religious group in California saying the world was going to end next month.

At the bottom of the pile was a thick envelope from the Bookfinder! Thick enough to hold five hundred dollars! He'd leave tomorrow. When Lou came home he'd be long gone. He'd call Jessica and tell her that he'd buy her a ticket and she could meet him in Chicago or somewhere. He tore open the envelope.

There was no check. Instead there was a two-page letter, typed single-space. He skimmed over the stuff at the beginning until he saw ". . . appears to be the edition in which my client is interested." Then he began to read more carefully.

> There is one more scene that is crucial and takes place on Blue Isle at a place called Sunset. Look for the statue of a cat with a kitten in its mouth.

Getting five hundred dollars was taking a lot of his time.

> Many years ago, a great storm caused over one hundred ships to be lost at sea, including the *Portland*, bound to Blue Isle from Boston. An islander had bought passage and was about to board when he saw a mother cat carrying her kittens, one by one, down the gangplank and off the ship. The man exchanged his ticket for a later sailing and arrived home safely a week later. The statue in question was erected in thanks to that cat.

Trevor thought it was a pretty good story. Maybe the Bookfinder should write his own books instead of buying them.

> One edition describes the statue as facing the bay; the other says it is facing the center of the island. We are interested in the accurate edition.

Trevor refolded the letter. Sunset? He ran up the stairs, two steps at a time, to find the map of the island Lou had given him along with the tide charts for the month.

It was easy to find the place on the map. The problem was that it would mean a fifteen-mile bike ride each way. What he'd better do first was find the description of the stone cat. He pulled Miranda York from under the bed, piled pillows against the headboard, leaned back, and began to read. He started a few pages back from where he'd stopped the last time.

Miranda York was brave and smart, and Flavia LaRue certainly knew a lot about smugglers. He could see the cove again—just as he and Ariel had found it a couple of days ago. He sat up straighter and read on.

Miranda York peered out into the darkness. Waves broke against the rocks far beneath, sending stray rippling across the narrow beach. Then came the flashing signals from the smugglers' boat. *Dit, dah, dit, dit.* She grew tense. "M-e-e-t c-a-t." The signals stopped. "Meet Cat," Miranda repeated. Who was Cat? Someone on the island?

Trevor punched up his pillows and switched on the bedside lamp.

It took Miranda York another six or seven pages before she figured out the strange message. There it finally was—the cat statue, "its back to the bay; its kitten in its mouth."

He stopped reading. If a statue like that was still standing at Sunset, the five hundred dollars was his. He checked his watch. It was almost seven and the sun was settling low over the Camden Hills. He'd never be able to get to Sunset and back before dark, even if he could pedal that far.

Freddie Ackerman, prisoner, smiled grimly, carefully closed the book, and hid it beneath his cot. His captors were gone, confident he was locked securely in his cell. Cautiously, he jimmied the locked door and stepped out into the darkened corridor, pausing to listen for the slightest sound. There was nothing but the ticking of a clock. Now for the Miata they'd carelessly left in the garage— with luck the keys would be in it.

He ran down the stairs. He'd never actually driven very far before. Charlie had let him back the car out of the driveway a few times, and once, when he was practicing his father routine, had even let Trevor drive around the block.

Trevor hesitated before he turned on the ignition. He checked out the lights, the dimmer, the brakes, and shifted through the gears. Nothing to it! The engine purred to life at the first turn of the key. He eased the car out of the garage, touched the brakes lightly, shifted into first, and headed to the main road. "Smooth as butter," Trevor whispered.

After the first mile or so, Trevor relaxed and glanced

in the rearview mirror. No one was following him and the road was empty ahead. He hit the accelerator and the tires squealed.

Once he'd turned west through the village, it wasn't hard to figure out when he arrived at Sunset. The road ended and the bay began. A wide parking area on one side held a dozen or so cars and pickups. Someone had a fire going on the beach and the sound of music—heavy metal—pounded over the shouts and laughter of what he guessed were high-school kids having a party.

It would have been fun to go over and watch, but he had more important things to do. He ran across the wet sand, attempting to avoid the globs of seaweed the tide had left on the beach. His sneakers soon filled with sand, but he kept on running until his legs felt like two lead weights. Flavia LaRue's six or seven pages were turning into half an hour. Where was the dumb statue? No wonder the smugglers decided to meet there. No one on the island would ever find it.

Suddenly, there it was, looming before him, a dark shadow silhouetted against the trees: a flat square of concrete well above the high-tide line, and on it the cat facing the center of the island! It was just what the Bookfinder wanted. Five hundred dollars were practically in Trevor's pocket!

He raced back along the shore toward Aunt Cal's car. He'd write the letter tonight, and by next week, at the very latest, he'd be rolling in dollars. Jessica always said money wasn't everything but it *was* the next best thing to a credit card. Maybe that's what he'd do—apply for his own credit card.

Then he saw the Blue Isle police car in the now-empty parking lot.

"Party's over, Trevor," Homer said, dangling Aunt Cal's car keys from one finger. "Don't suppose there's any point in asking to see your driver's license, is there?"

"Probably not," Trevor said, shrugging.

"And I don't suppose Miss Calla knows you borrowed her car, does she?"

"I wasn't at the party, though." Trevor tried to think of what the attorneys on "LA Law" called extenuating circumstances.

"Good thing you weren't. Otherwise we'd have to run you in with the rest of those kids and you'd be in even bigger trouble than you are now. What do you suppose your aunts would do if you were caught in a beer bust?"

Trevor couldn't even begin to imagine.

Homer opened the door and climbed behind the wheel. "We'll make real sure that you and your aunt's car get home safe and sound. My deputy will follow us back to Skyfield."

When they pulled up in front of the house, Trevor blinked, closed his eyes tightly, opened them, and blinked again. Lou was walking toward them, her robe floating in the night breeze.

"Lost, strayed, or stolen, Homer?" She wasn't smiling, but she wasn't yelling either.

"A little of each, I'd say, but I'll let you sort that out, Miss Lou. A policeman's work is never done." He turned and looked down at Trevor. "This is number two. Three strikes and you're out. Right, boy?"

Trevor couldn't shake his head or even nod, so he stared at the ground and tried to figure out how many weeks were left in the summer that he'd have to spend with the *its*.

"Right," Lou answered for him. "Thank you, Homer, for your time and trouble. And you, Trevor, might as well put your aunt's car away. If you could get it to Sunset, you can drive it into the garage."

By the time he returned, Homer had left, but Lou was waiting. He wanted to ask how she knew where he'd been, but he'd had enough experience with his various parents to be sure asking questions wasn't smart.

"Classy little number, isn't it? The car, I mean," Lou said.

He looked at her for the first time. "It sure is." He remembered how it felt sitting behind the wheel, surrounded by the smell of leather, and in command of all that power.

"It's a rule of the universe, Trevor, that every effect has a cause, and, conversely, every cause has its effect."

She sounded a little bit like Stensrud the Philosopher.

"Now, what would be the worst effect that might result from this affair?" She leaned toward him.

"You mean what should you do to me?" he asked.

"What would be the worst thing I could do?"

"Call my real father."

"We can't do that. Our phone bill is a bit steep this month. What would be next worst?"

"Send me to Bermuda?"

Lou shook her head. "Too expensive. Try again."

Trevor was glad it was dark. Otherwise Lou would think he had a fever, if his face was as red as it felt. "Tell Aunt Cal," he muttered.

"Exactly!" Her voice was triumphant. She started slowly toward the house, then turned and spoke as if she were confiding a special secret. "Problems with drivers' licenses seem to run in the family, and I don't think we should bother Calla with either of our little driving problems, do you?"

He certainly didn't.

"Since you're so fond of the car," she went on, "to-morrow you may vacuum it, wash it, wax it, and polish it—we'll consider it a welcome-home gift for your aunt when she arrives." She opened the screen door. "Now, let's go to bed. It's been a long day for both of us."

Even though it was long past his bedtime, Trevor sat at his desk and wrote what he hoped would be his last letter to the Bookfinder. Maybe five hundred dollars would buy a used car. When he was driving, Freddie Ackerman had been handsome, confident, in control. Trevor wouldn't mind feeling like that *all* the time.

When he finally finished everything he wanted to tell the Bookfinder, he realized he'd again written a much longer letter than he'd intended. He'd wanted to describe everything in detail—how the statue was almost six feet high, carved out of gray stone, and how Freddie had to borrow a car in order to get to Sunset, and how beautiful it was when the water turned red, as if on fire.

THE NEXT MORNING, Lou met him as he was on his way
to the pink Schwinn, the letter in his pocket.

"You can back the car out and begin." She settled in
a lawn chair beside the garage. "I got this instruction
manual for the driver's license test I'll have to take. While
you do the car, I'll study."

That suited him fine, except that Lou didn't study;
she watched, eagle-eyed, as he vacuumed and washed
and polished. Then she worked a crossword puzzle, and
once when he looked up, she had her eyes closed. It took
him most of the morning, and he was beginning to think
he'd never get free so he could mail his letter.

"Nice job, Trevor," she said, sounding as if she meant
it. The car did look great when he finished, its chrome
glistening and the green so deep and shiny it set off spar-

kles wherever the sunlight hit it. "Now you might bike into the village for the mail. When you get back, I'd like you to ask me the sample questions for the test."

He almost laughed. She hadn't spent more than ten minutes out of the whole morning studying the manual. She'd never pass the test, not in a million years.

Later, sitting on the sun porch, the manual in his hand, he stopped laughing as he read, "What is the shape of a stop sign?"

"Octagon."

"What is the shape of a yield sign?"

"Triangle."

She breezed through the road signs; recited, word for word, the speed limits for residential, school, and business zones and the passing limits to exact number of feet; and, for good measure, repeated verbatim the rest of the questions before Trevor had a chance to ask them.

"How did you do that?" She must have cheated. Maybe she had invisible ink on the backs of her hands.

"Photographic memory. I was born with it. What I read or hear can stick in my mind like bugs on flypaper, though I suppose you're too young to know what flypaper is."

"Could I learn how to do it?" Trevor had a brief and beautiful vision of floating through the rest of his education with a quick look and listen.

"I don't think it's teachable, and I'm not sure it's learnable, but maybe it's in your genes. You *are* family, after all."

Family genes sounded like sharing a pair of Levi's. "Do you have to practice, like doing push-ups?"

"No, it's just there—like breathing. It's time to get over to the mainland and take the test. Do you want to come with me? It shouldn't take long."

He did and it didn't.

Trevor sat in the back of the room and watched Lou fill in the blanks with her number two pencil, barely taking the time to read the test questions before she selected answers. She was finished long before the others who were taking the exam, yet she made no move to turn in her paper.

Finally a skinny blond who must have been getting her very first license stood up, handed in her test, and then, upon an order from the uniformed examiner, peered into the vision machine.

"*H G X I E,*" the girl intoned.

Lou leaned forward.

"*C D B N M,*" the girl continued. She must have done well, because the examiner smiled and pointed toward the photographer.

Lou stood up and hurried to the desk.

"Read the third line down, please."

Standing on tiptoe, Lou looked into the machine. "*H G X I E.*"

"You don't wear glasses?"

"Certainly not," Lou said.

"Try the fourth line down, then."

"*C D B N M.*" Her voice was full of confidence.

"Very good! And you passed the written test." She looked at Lou again. "We don't see many of these—a perfect score. You certainly did your homework."

"Discipline," Lou explained.

After the photo-taking and signature, the examiner handed Lou the license. "Your license is good for one year—after this."

"Discrimination," Lou muttered to Trevor as they left. "Now I need to stop at a drugstore. It'll just take a minute."

It took much longer than a minute, and when she finally emerged, she wore a pair of horn-rimmed glasses that made her look like a creature from outer space.

"Why did you buy those?" Trevor asked. "You passed the vision test."

"That was thanks to my audio, not my visual. After the first line I couldn't see a thing, so I just repeated what that girl read. I do think I've pushed my luck far enough, though. These glasses *do* make a difference. I can see the speedometer!"

On the way back to Blue Isle, Trevor asked, "How come you didn't go to a real eye doctor?"

Lou snorted. "Opthalmologists cost money; drugstores are cheap, and either way, I'd still end up with glasses."

Maybe Lou was so poor that she couldn't afford real glasses the same way she couldn't afford a new car. It was crazy, though, because Aunt Cal had to be rich to drive a Miata.

When they got home, Lou stopped him on the way to the house. "Your aunt will be home one of these days, and she'll probably be worn out, so—"

"So there's no reason to tell her about the exam, right?" Trevor finished the sentence.

"You're learning fast. I couldn't have said it better myself. You and I have more in common than I could have guessed."

"It probably runs in our genes," Trevor said. When the words came out they were more serious than he'd meant them to be.

Even if Trevor had intended to tell Aunt Cal about Lou's exam, he couldn't have. Melva met her plane, Aunt Cal swooped in amid luggage and packages and books, and there definitely was no room in the one-woman conversation for anyone but Lou to insert an occasional, "How nice! You don't say!"

"A success? Louisa, you wouldn't believe it unless you were there. I met so many people! Hardly any time to sleep! Lavishly entertained everywhere! And such food—not that I ate a bite of it." She fell back in her chair and glanced at Trevor. " 'I am old and foolish.' That is *King Lear*, Act IV."

"You're not foolish. You just had fun."

"Trevor, you have a way with words. We have more in common than I imagined."

He didn't say that it probably ran in the family, but he thought it.

The next letter from the Bookfinder arrived a few days

later. Without saying a word, Lou tossed it into his lap as he sat on the steps trying to figure, if he went to Las Vegas, how long five hundred dollars would last if he spent ten dollars a day playing the slots, and maybe five dollars in the pop machine. He couldn't decide whether it would take thirty days or three hundred days. It was hard to divide in his head. It was easier to add.

He stuck the letter in his back pocket and walked slowly toward the bay and across the stones that led to Lost Island. No one ever disturbed him when he was on the little island. It was like walking into another world.

Freddie Ackerman, famed special agent, sat beneath the giant tree on the secluded atoll, the envelope tucked beneath his shirt. He quickly scanned the surroundings, alert for the sound of footsteps. Hearing nothing, he pulled the communiqué out and held it for a moment before opening it. If all was well, this envelope would hold the answer to his quest.

He drew a deep breath and opened it. He knew, as he unfolded the letter, that there was no money inside. He scanned the page. More instructions! Not again!

". . . excellent job. One last request . . . the ransom money that Miranda York pretends to leave behind the loose brick of the Inn's fireplace. Does reality match fiction? If so, you may have a first edition, which should certainly be worth $500."

He studied the title at the bottom of the letter: Book-finder. Trevor could see the old man sitting in his dusty second-hand bookstore, peering at the wall, dreaming up another errand for Freddie Ackerman. Thinking of another excuse not to send five hundred dollars right away.

A loose brick in the Inn's fireplace? The Bookfinder must have more than one brick loose himself. How was Freddie Ackerman supposed to get into a place like that? So far, the closest Trevor had come to it was viewing it from the front of Will's Groceries. His aunts played Scrabble with the owners, he remembered, but he didn't think they would let him go in and grope around their fireplace.

Trevor folded the letter, stuck it in his pocket, and, closing his eyes, leaned back against the big tree. Of course, he could lie. He could write back and pretend he'd found the stupid brick. It was, though, kind of interesting to find out if all the things Miranda York saw really existed. Besides, it was bad enough to sell Aunt Cal's book, even if she didn't want it, without trying to con the Bookfinder.

"Are you asleep?" Her voice was right in his ear.

"Of course not." He hadn't heard her walk toward him. "How did you know where I was?"

"Miss Lou told me." Ariel sat down beside him. "What are you doing out here?"

"Thinking." It was funny, but every time he saw her, she looked different, and also cuter somehow.

"Thinking about what?" She smelled sweet.

"Thinking about what I should do."

"I never think about what I *should* do, I just do it.

That saves a lot of time. I suppose it's because of the hormonal difference between girls and boys. I think we have more of them. Or maybe the other way around."

He wasn't quite sure about hormones, but he hoped he had the right amount.

"See, if you're a girl, you never know how boys will be one minute to the next. Sometimes they're totally human, and the next minute they turn into dorks. I suppose you know that because you are one. A boy, not a dork. At least not right now."

Sometimes being with Ariel was like listening to a tape on fast reverse.

She leaned back against the tree. "Do you come out here often?"

"Just when I have decisions to make." He could feel the letter in his pocket.

"What kind of decisions?"

"About life. Whether I should go out for soccer next year. Important stuff like that." He wondered what she'd think about the Bookfinder.

"It's probably because of where we're sitting," she said. "A place like this is special. We're right on top of the lovers, remember? Their spirits must be all around us."

"Only a twerk could believe in lovers and spirits and stuff like that." He wanted to swallow the words, but they were already out in the air.

"I'm no twerk!" Ariel scrambled to her feet. "And you have the imagination of a quark. Some things need to be believed."

He hurried after her. "I believe! I believe! It was just my hormones running around."

She let him catch up with her. "Probably," she answered as the breeze ruffled her hair into wisps of gold. "I wonder where they live. In our stomachs or in our heads?"

Trevor didn't know. All he was sure of was that his stomach felt light and his brain felt heavy. "Let's bike to the village. I'll split a cola with you." She didn't look convinced, so he added, "We'll trade bikes!"

By the time they coasted past the post office, Trevor knew his hormones were gasping for breath. Trying to keep up with Ariel as he pedaled her old Hiawatha was like trying to fly carrying lead weights.

Sitting on a boulder beside the millpond, Trevor pointed toward the Inn. "Have you ever been inside there?" He wasn't trying to use her. It wasn't as if he'd planned this. Ariel just happened to be around.

"Sure. Everybody has. It goes back to the Revolutionary War, back to when Blue Isle was settled."

"It has a lot of chimneys." He hoped that each one didn't mean a separate fireplace. "What's it like inside?"

"Well, you go in that big wooden door in front and then there's a wide hall with big beams and a smooth stone floor." If he closed his eyes, he could imagine it was Miranda York talking.

"What about fireplaces?" He didn't care about stone floors.

"There are three or four downstairs and maybe some

upstairs, too. You go down the hall like this." Her fore-finger traced the route on the surface of the rock. "If you turn here, there's the lobby, and it has a fireplace with an opening higher than your head. You could roast a whole steer in it."

Trevor wondered how many bricks were in *that* chimney.

"Across this hall there's another room with a fireplace the same size. That room has glass doors that open onto the lawn. Then there's another fireplace at the end of *this* hall."

It was impossible, Trevor decided. He'd write the Bookfinder and ask if he had any idea how many bricks there were to search through. He didn't really need the five hundred dollars anyway. If he could get enough money for bus fare to Bangor, he could cash in his own plane ticket and go anywhere he wanted. All he had to do was sell the Walkman, and he hadn't been using it much lately anyway.

Ariel was still explaining the floor plan of the Inn. She sounded like the computerized voice in the airport that kept up the persistent monotone about "no smoking except in designated areas."

"I have to go," he finally said, climbing off the rock and picking up the Schwinn.

Ariel stopped talking.

"There are a bunch of things that I have to do." He didn't understand why he was bothering to explain.

"Like what? If you want to go inside the Inn, I'll show

you. Come on." She held out her hand and for just a moment he touched her fingers before she let go. Ariel had warm fingers.

"I can't," he said. "I told you I have stuff to do. Boy stuff," he added. Why did he say things like that to her? He really wanted to tell her all about the Bookfinder and the five hundred dollars and how Blue Isle wasn't quite so boring when *she* was around, but he didn't know how to begin.

It was easier just to get on the bike and pedal away. When he looked back, Ariel was standing, hands on her hips, watching him.

Back at Skyfield, because there was nothing else to do, he pulled out *Steps on the Stairs* again and looked up the part about the fireplace. Curled up in the window seat, he propped the book against his knees.

Miranda York felt carefully along the surface of the west chimney, searching for the loose brick. The air was heavy with the tang of the sea, and the grass beneath her bare feet—

Trevor dropped the book. The loose brick was outside, not inside! And Miranda even explained which chimney it was. If he had Lou's photographic memory, he'd have known right away.

He was almost positive of one thing. Instead of waiting until he got home to buy a hot-pink Yamaha Razz moped, he'd buy it here just as soon as the check arrived. He'd even take Ariel for a ride on it, just in case she was mad at him for biking off and leaving her. Besides, if he already had it, his mother couldn't very well object. Of course, he'd have to find out how much it would cost to ship it home.

It was almost midnight before Trevor heard Lou go down the hall to her half of Skyfield. The stereo clicked downstairs as Aunt Cal turned off the piano concerto she'd been listening to. He knew it was a concerto because the first night she played the tape, she told him more about it than he ever wanted to know.

He found the bike where he'd stashed it earlier, down by the main road. The stars and moon were hidden by threatening black clouds that seemed to almost touch the treetops. A car passed him when he was pedaling hard up the last steep hill, its lights pushing his shadow out ahead of him on the road.

It would have been fun to have Ariel with him, but he remembered what Other-Father-Norman said the day he moved out: "He travels fastest who travels alone." Next to "Never give a sucker an even break," that had been Norman's favorite line.

Trevor coasted past the post office, past Will's store, and down to the big rock where he'd sat with Ariel. A couple of the upper rooms of the Inn were lit, but otherwise the place was dark except for a dim light above the front door.

Leaving his bike, he crept to the back of the Inn, moved silently down its length, and peeked around the corner. The west chimney jutted out from the rest of the building. He thought he heard something, but after he was sure it was only his imagination, he slid around the corner and made his way to the chimney.

"Two in from the right," he whispered. "Eleven up from the ground."

Something was planted at the base of the chimney. He couldn't tell where the brick was so that he could start counting. He switched on his flashlight. He was standing up to his ankles in a flower bed. Trevor started to count, moving his hand up and across each brick.

"Four . . . five . . . six." He stood and continued the count. "Ten . . . eleven." The brick moved under the weight of his hand. He dropped the flashlight and slipped the brick from its place.

Without intending to, he pushed his free hand into the hole and felt something soft, slippery, and heavy. He pulled the package free of its resting place, let go of the brick, and stooped to pick up the flashlight.

"Don't move!" Homer's voice wasn't loud, but it was fierce, and Trevor froze.

"Now, turn around slowly and keep your hands away from your body." In the darkness, Trevor's discarded flashlight shone on a trampled peony.

He felt Homer moving toward him across the lawn. Still clutching the plastic bag, Trevor turned, an inch at a time until he was blinded by a bright beam of light. He swallowed hard a couple of times, hoping Homer wouldn't count that as movement.

The light flicked off as Homer stood beside him. "I should have known it was you, Trevor Ackerman. Just where you shouldn't be and just when you shouldn't be there."

Trevor thought about saying it was the story of his entire life. Instead, he held out the plastic bag. "I found this." Now that his eyes had readjusted to the darkness, he could see Homer scowling at him.

"Of course, you found *this*. It was meant to be found. But it wasn't *Trevor* who was supposed to find it. I know who put it there, and I've been waiting every night for the past week for somebody to pick it up. And who do I find?"

The answer was obvious, so Trevor gave it. "Me, I guess. It's coke, isn't it?" This was even better than Miranda York.

"It's coke, all right, and it's going back where you found it. I'm not even going to ask what you're doing here, or how you knew that was the only loose brick in the whole blame chimney. I don't think I'd believe it if I heard it." He shoved the package into the empty space and pushed the brick back into place.

"It was kind of an accident." Homer had sounded so upset that Trevor wanted to explain so that he'd feel better. "I read about it in a book. The chimney, I mean, not the drugs. And I wanted to know if the hiding place was really there."

"Pick up your flashlight and come with me." Homer sounded a little as if he was choking on something. "If no one saw us, there's still a chance this will work."

As they rounded the corner of the Inn, Homer asked, "Was that you on the bike that I passed a little while ago on the road?"

"I guess it must have been," Trevor said.

"Do you realize, Trevor Ackerman, that I could arrest you not only for trespassing, interfering with an officer in his line of duty, trampling a flower garden, but *also* for riding a bicycle with no reflectors at night on a public highway?" Homer stopped for air.

"No." Trevor was impressed. "I didn't realize all that."

Homer pulled off his police cap and scratched his head. "Tell you what I'm going to do. I'll take you and your bike back to Skyfield and drop you off at the end of the drive so we don't wake your aunts. *You* are going to forget this ever happened. *You* will not mention this trap to a single, solitary, living soul. In other words, Trevor Ackerman, this will be our little secret!"

On the way home, Trevor stayed busy trying to remember all the secrets he was supposed to forget. It was turning out to be a very busy summer after all.

CAREFULLY AVOIDING the two steps that creaked when he put his weight on them, Trevor crept slowly up the stairs. In his room, he undressed in the dark, slid into bed, and, in the middle of a yawn, heard a door click shut.

Someone must have heard him. He'd have to come up with a believable excuse that didn't include Homer. The whole idea of Homer's staking out a drug stash wasn't too believable anyway. He fell asleep and dreamed of bags of white powder floating in the sky above the Inn like fluffy white clouds.

He woke suddenly to a brilliant flash of lightning followed by a hiss, crackle, and a clap of thunder that rattled every window in his bedroom. Minutes later a flashlight shone against the wall and Aunt Cal towered beside his bed.

"You're awake, aren't you, Trevor? Bring a blanket and come on downstairs with us. There's no electricity. Our transformer must have been hit again."

"Where are we going?" he asked, trying to remember instructions about where to hide in a storm.

"Out here." The flashlight pointed to the sun porch. "It's the best view in the house."

Lou was hunched near a partially open window that let splatters of raindrops through. Candles flickered from the coffee table as gusts of wind made weird shadows dance across the walls.

"What took you so long?" She laughed. "You almost missed the exciting part. Sit here, Trevor." Lou motioned to a cushion on the floor near her chair. "You can see better by the window."

The wind swept in from the bay, whipping sheets of rain that scudded across the lawn, snapping off tree branches and beating Aunt Cal's flowers into the ground. The thunder became a steady roar, with lightning turning the night into flashes of day, trees silhouetted against the churning storm clouds.

Aunt Cal sank into her chair, arranged a blanket over her knees, and surveyed the scene as if giving permission for the storm to continue.

"Don't you love storms?" Lou said as a sudden gust of wind bent the ornamental shrubs to the ground.

"Not at night," Trevor mumbled, pulling his blanket around his shoulders.

Through the open window he could smell the wind, heavy with rain, and hear the crash of water against the rocks in the cove. He was glad he wasn't in his bedroom. He was even gladder that he wasn't biking home from the Inn. His aunts looked as if they were watching a play, and when lightning struck the shoreline, he almost expected them to applaud.

"Remember, Calla," Lou turned away from the window, "how Papa used to bring us down here on nights like this to see how long it was between the thunder and the lightning? Your grandmother and I, Trevor, shut our eyes and hid under our blankets. Calla stood right beside Papa and counted out loud. She was never afraid."

"I was always afraid." Aunt Cal's voice was soft. "I just pretended not to be."

Lou turned back to the window. "I thought you loved storms."

"I do now, but that's only because I've lived through so many. Now I *am* waving, *not* drowning. That's one of your aunt's favorite poems, Trevor. She wishes she'd written it herself."

"Stevie Smith beat me to it. And your aunt has the name of the poem backward because she's making what is called a literary allusion or, in this case, perhaps, an illusion. The poem," she continued, "is about a man who dies in the ocean because no one realizes he's in trouble. The last two lines are 'I was much too far out all my life / And not waving but drowning."

Trevor shivered. He wasn't sure whether it was because of the sound of Lou's voice or the lightning that struck somewhere out in the cove.

The storm raged on until, as Lou predicted, it blew itself out, leaving only a soft drip of rain from tree branches and a faraway rumble of thunder. Lou opened all the windows, and the air, freshly laundered, poured in, filling the room with sweetness.

"The best is over," Aunt Cal announced. "I'm going to bed. Are you two coming?"

"We'll stay up a little longer," Lou answered. "I'll see that Trevor finds his way back to his room." She looked down at him. "You're not tired, are you?"

"Not very." He yawned.

"You must be a night person like me."

She'd heard him come home. He knew it. It had been her door that clicked shut. He was also pretty sure she wouldn't ask anything out loud, but the question would be there, hanging unspoken between them.

"Calla used to be a night person, too, but as one grows older . . . I guess I can't say *older*. We're already old! Melva says that soon we'll have to go down to Florida to find enough pallbearers to bury us." Lou chuckled.

Trevor didn't like to think about pallbearers and things like that when the darkness had now grown so heavy he could hear it filtering through the treetops and wrapping itself around the house.

"I worry about Calla," Lou went on. "I tell her to lose weight. She says people are supposed to get fatter when they grow old so that they can fill out their wrinkles." She laughed again.

This time Trevor grinned.

"Lately, she's been working too hard. She claims it takes longer to come up with a fresh idea. I say it's cholesterol cloggage."

"Does she have to work so hard?" Maybe she was short of money, after all, even if she did drive an expensive car. Maybe that was why she and Lou lived together and why she was so excited about somebody paying for her plane ticket to go to New York. He tried to forget about the five hundred dollars he'd be getting in just a week or so.

"Calla's work is her life," Lou answered after a long silence. "She never married, you know. She might have, but he was lost at sea during World War Two."

Trevor squeezed his eyes shut and thought of Freddie Ackerman, the young naval officer lost at sea, waving as his destroyer went down and drowning as he dreamed of Aunt Cal.

He was glad when Lou finally said, "I think we two ought to get to sleep, or there'll be no night left."

He woke to bright sunlight streaming into his windows and to voices echoing up from the lawn. He groped his way across the room and looked out. The storm had littered the grass with fallen tree limbs, uprooted shrubs, and torn, muddy leaves. Down near the shore stood his aunts, Melva and—Ariel! What was she doing here so early in the morning?

He looked where Aunt Cal was pointing, rubbed his

eyes, and looked again. The tree that had stood so tall on Lost Island lay uprooted, its top half-hidden in the water, its roots torn and exposed, hanging in a mass of mud above an ugly black hole.

Trevor felt the way he had that last day of school when Jessica turned from her locker and shouted so everyone in the hall could hear what she called him. That was how he felt now, looking at the smashed tree.

He hurried to dress, and by the time he reached the cove, Homer had arrived with a screech of brakes and lights flashing. He was marking off the path to Lost Island with yellow tape as if it were the scene of a crime. Maybe the drug bust had happened right here!

"What's going on?" Trevor asked as he stood beside Ariel.

"There are two skeletons out there in that hole." She looked at him the way Jessica always did when she got an A and he got a C. "Miss Lou discovered them first thing this morning, and they're just like I told you—in each other's arms right where they took the poison. You didn't believe me, did you?"

"I believed you." He added under his breath, "Sort of."

"Homer says we have to stay here and wait for the state archaeologist."

"You mean we can't go look until he comes?"

"He's a she." Ariel was looking superior.

"Who's a she?"

"The archaeologist, of course."

She didn't arrive until early the next morning, accompanied by two helpers. Ariel was close behind, pedaling hard to keep up with their van.

"They're not to be disturbed," Aunt Cal warned as they watched the woman and her crew unload shovels, trowels, brushes, and plastic bags and carry them out to Lost Island. "We can watch from here."

"What's Lou doing out there?" Trevor asked. She had met the van when it arrived and followed the crew out to the island.

"She's taking pictures for the newspaper. She writes a column for the *Island Eagle*."

"I *always* read her column," Ariel piped up. "She's very creative."

He knew she was trying to figure out a way to sneak over there, past the yellow tape.

"I've got to get to work," Aunt Cal said. "Let me know if anything exciting happens."

Ariel sprawled out on the grass. "You're really lucky to be on our island when all this is happening."

"Big deal!" She was just trying to remind him that he didn't belong here the way she did. "They're probably just some old animal bones left over from somebody's dinner." He sat down beside her.

"You really *are* a quark, Trevor Ackerman. You're so unoriginal, I'll bet you don't even dream." She didn't bother to look at him.

"And you don't know the difference between a hole in the ground and a hole in your head." He wasn't sure why he was being so mean.

"Verrry funny!" Ariel stood up and started toward the path that had been cordoned off. "You know something, Trevor? Sometimes you're . . . you're . . ." Her voice trailed off until she was almost to the trees. Then she shouted, "You're terribly hard to like!"

He watched until she reappeared beyond the yellow tape. He'd forget about her and the stupid bones. He'd go inside and write to the Bookfinder. At least Ariel wouldn't bother him there.

He got out stationery and pen and began with "Dear Sir," but he didn't feel much like being polite or business-like. "I found the loose brick, so you can send me—" That sounded greedy. "My book—" only it wasn't *his* book.

He put down the pen. It was Aunt Cal's book. Maybe he could give her part of the money and still have enough left to buy a Windsurfer. That wasn't such a great idea, though, because Real-Father didn't take him to the beach very often, and with the *its* along, there wouldn't be enough room to haul it.

Freddie Ackerman, commanding general of the Allied forces, pondered what lay ahead. Tomorrow he would lead his men into the last great battle of the war. He would be at the head of his troops, an act that could mean his death. He recalled the vow he had sworn: to keep himself physically strong, mentally awake, and morally straight. There was one last act he must undertake.

He took out a clean sheet of stationery and wrote: "Dear Mr. Bookfinder: I am sorry, but the book *Steps on the Stairs* does not belong to me, so I can't sell it to you." He signed "T. Freddie Ackerman," folded the sheet, inserted it into the envelope, and stamped it. He'd mail it tomorrow.

Then he did something that surprised him even more than writing the letter. He went to Aunt Cal's library, pulled out the A volume of the encyclopedia, looked up archaeology, curled up in a chair, and began to read.

Under the burning Egyptian sun of a late autumn day in 1922, a group of archaeologists made their way slowly down into the Valley of the Tombs of Kings.

It wasn't Miranda York, but it was interesting. He read about somebody called King Tutankhamen, about the Rosetta Stone buried under the sand, about stone tools, and finally about the discovery of a prehistoric man.

He'd finished archaeology and started on architecture when Aunt Cal burst into the room. "Did you hear the noise outside? What's going on?"

Trevor hadn't heard anything. "I'll go see," he offered before she could ask what he was doing in her library in the middle of the morning.

He was almost across the lawn when he saw them—

the archaeologist, Lou and . . . Ariel! She wasn't grinning and triumphant, though. She was walking slowly, her mouth a stubborn little slit.

Trevor jogged up to her. "What goes?"

She kept walking and didn't answer right away.

She looked as if she wanted to cry. "It's all wrong."

They'd reached the corner of the house. He never knew how to act when people looked as if they wanted to cry. Mostly they said, "Just leave me alone," but with Ariel, he wasn't sure.

He reached out to touch her shoulder so that she'd at least look at him, but at that very moment, she spun around and his hand clipped her a whop right on the chin.

"I didn't hurt you, did I? I wouldn't do that!" Why, when he was acting adult—he'd seen a guy on TV do that, reach out and touch a girl—did it always turn out wrong?

Ariel didn't yell at him, or cry, either. She leaned against the house and looked up at the sky. "It was all wrong. It was all so sad."

"You mean the lovers?" He said the word seriously. "There weren't any bones after all?"

"There were skeletons lying together, but they weren't lovers." She swiped at her eyes with the back of one hand. "They were two men who killed each other. The big one had a stone knife between his ribs and the small one's neck was broken. It was awful."

Trevor took a very deep breath while he hunted for

words. This moment, for some crazy reason, felt more important than anything that had ever happened to him—even losing *Lark*. He stared up where Ariel was looking, the pine branches black-green against the bright sky. "I think it's okay to believe what you hope is true." He wondered where the words came from and waited to hear what Freddie Ackerman would say next. "And maybe the truth isn't as important as what might be."

At first, when Ariel looked at him, he thought she was going to laugh, but she didn't. Instead, *she* reached over and touched *his* face. "Trevor Ackerman, I take it back. Sometimes you're not at all hard to like."

·*10*·

TREVOR WAS IN THE MIDDLE of his second set of push-ups when he heard Ariel's signal. She could stick two fingers in her mouth and whistle so loudly it almost split his eardrums. She'd asked if he'd like to bike down to Stoneport that morning.

"A lot of kids from school hang out down there," she'd said.

"Do you ride down there often?"

"Whenever I feel like it."

"Are those kids really friends of yours?"

"Sure. I thought you might like them."

He'd thought so, too, except that he'd forgotten all about Stoneport.

As he wheeled the Schwinn toward her, he noticed

she was wearing a new pair of white shorts and a frilly blouse, and she'd caught her hair up in a scarflike thing that made him pay attention to her face. She looked older somehow, as if she'd grown up since he last saw her.

Before he got on his bike, he asked, "Will there be some guys down there?"

"Guys? You mean boys?" She frowned at him. "Why? Are you allergic to girls all of a sudden?"

"Don't be dumb. I was just curious."

She stood still, balancing her bike. "Kids come and go. It depends on whether they have summer jobs or not."

"What are their names?" He wanted to tell her not to say his was Trevor, to call him Freddie Ackerman instead. Kids with names like Mike and Rick and Butch could make things tough for a Trevor. Jessica said it was because they could pronounce only one syllable at a time.

Ariel looked at him, her eyebrows raised, and didn't answer.

"Come on! Name one!" It wasn't because he felt uncomfortable, it was because he was sure she was lying that his voice was so loud. She'd admitted she let the air out of his tire so that he'd talk to her. He'd bet anything that she didn't have a single friend. "You can't name one, can you?" he shouted, as he hopped onto his bike and sped to the end of the lane.

He was almost to the road when he noticed Ariel wasn't following him. She hadn't moved. Trevor turned around and rode back to her. "You don't have any friends down there, do you?" It seemed important to make her admit it.

She looked directly at him. Her eyes were greener in the shade than in the sunlight. "Sure I do, but if you want to find some guys, go ahead. See if I care." Her eyes were even greener when she was mad. "Anyway, I have something to do for Aunt Melva at the library."

"What?" She had to be lying.

"She has a book she wants me to take to Miss Calla as a surprise—a book she's been trying hard to find."

"Your Aunt Melva?"

"No, bubble-brain! *Your* aunt."

"What for?" Ariel had lost him.

"Your aunt's a book dealer, Trevor." Her voice was so patient he wanted to strangle her. "In case you didn't know, people write from all over asking her to locate books. She gets so much mail that she has to have a special address in New York City."

Trevor didn't want to hear any more, but Ariel kept talking.

"She calls herself the Bookfinder and—"

Trevor felt sick. A burning started in his stomach and moved up to his throat. "I don't believe it!" His words came out in a little-boy squeak. "You're lying! You lie about everything."

For a minute, Trevor thought she was going to paste him one. Instead, she yanked up the kickstand of her bike, and, looking him straight in the eyes, she said, emphasizing each word, "I only lied to you once, Trevor Ackerman. That was when I told you I spend the winter with my mother in Bangor. I live with Grandpa all the time, and I do too have friends in Stoneport."

She straddled the bike and started pedaling. "And for your information," she shouted over her shoulder, "I don't *have* a mother!" She turned toward the village.

Trevor felt even sicker. Jessica would call it "puke-sick." He wasn't sure if it was because of how he'd treated Ariel or what she'd told him about Aunt Cal. He thought of all those stupid letters he'd sent the Bookfinder. Lou must have read them, too.

Another thought began to form, and he put his head down between his knees. All summer he'd been running around the island searching for stuff that was in the book, and it was his aunts who had sent him. They'd been laughing at him for weeks.

Maybe Ariel was making it all up, but he didn't think so. In fact, he didn't really want to think about her at all because he was ashamed of himself. What he'd said to her was a whole lot worse than anything Jessica had shouted at him. He'd kill himself, except that on Blue Isle, suicide was redundant.

He finally got back on his bike. This was supposed to have been a fun day—riding with Ariel to the tip of the island—and now she'd spoiled everything. That wasn't true. *He'd* spoiled it all by himself. Ariel had ridden toward the village, so he'd go the other way.

Ten minutes into his ride, he was ready to turn

around. Being alone made him feel worse and worse. He hadn't brought his Walkman, so there was nothing to do but think. Even having Ariel yell at him would be better than this. He cut a half circle and headed back to Skyfield.

He was almost there when Ariel came flying toward him, not coasting, but pedaling as fast as she could.

"Trevor!" she shouted. "It's your aunt!" She nearly fell off the bike as she braked to a stop. "Her car's in the ditch and they've taken her away."

He knew Ariel was telling the truth. Her face was as pale as her hair.

"Is she hurt?" He tried to swallow, but his mouth was so dry he could hardly move his tongue. He could imagine the Miata upside down, its hood smashed.

"I don't know. Homer has the place roped off, and I met the ambulance." Ariel's voice shook.

Aunt Cal couldn't die—she was too big and too . . . alive. Besides, he wasn't sure Lou could live without her, even though they argued sometimes. Freddie Ackerman would know what to do, but Trevor couldn't find him.

"We'd better get back to Skyfield." Ariel had already turned her bike around.

He was glad she'd said "we." He didn't want to go alone.

News of the accident must have spread because cars sped past them, probably on the way to see what had happened. Other-Father-Norman had been like that if they came across an accident. He'd slow down and even stop to look. Trevor had always turned the other way.

The driveway was empty when they wheeled up to the garage, but Melva met them at the door.

"How is she?" Trevor's voice came out in little jerks.

"Bumped and bruised, but otherwise fine. She's in the library."

Trevor tiptoed down the hall, through the fireplace room, and peeked into the library. Aunt Cal stood by the window, and sitting on the couch sipping tea was Lou, a bandage across one temple.

It wasn't the green Miata, it was the old station wagon! And it wasn't Aunt Cal, it was Lou!

"What happened?" He should have thought of his aunts before the cars. He felt his neck redden and hoped no one could read his mind. "Are you hurt?" he hurried to add.

"No brain, no pain." Aunt Cal sniffed as she turned from the window.

Lou put down her cup. "I was merely thinking of something else."

"Obviously!" Aunt Cal sounded angry. "Your mind certainly wasn't on your driving."

"To tell the truth, Calla, I was trying to think of a word to rhyme with *mulch*."

"*Mulch?*" echoed Aunt Cal.

"Yes, *mulch*. And I had just thought of one when— whoops! There was the S curve right in front of me. It was too late to S, so I closed my eyes, hung on, and started reciting the Declaration of Independence."

"Louisa! The what?" Aunt Cal shouted.

Lou closed her eyes and recited, " 'When in the course of human events, it becomes necessary for one person . . .' "

"I think it's 'one people,' Louisa." Aunt Cal walked over and felt Lou's head.

"In my case, it was one person. That's as far as I got, and over I went. I can't think of that word now to save me. I guess it was knocked right out of my head." She started to laugh and then stopped and touched the bandage.

"Was the word for one of your poems?" Ariel, who had stayed behind in the hallway, joined Trevor and looked down at Lou as if she were a queen.

"The card was for someone you'd love a lot. There was to be this big red rose growing in a garden, and a verse to say, in effect, 'I chose this rose because I love you.' Then when you opened the card, the punch line would be, 'But you'll never know how mulch.' "

"You wrecked a car for that!" Aunt Cal groaned and then went on, "At least you're rid of that wretched station wagon. There wasn't a road on the island wide enough for that monster. Anyone meeting you had to take the shoulder."

"Maybe the word was *gulch*," Ariel suggested. "You could say the rose grew in a gulch"

"*Gulch?*" Lou nodded slowly. "*Gulch,*" she repeated. "Could be, but it's not a pretty word, is it?" She smiled at Ariel. "Some words, no matter what they mean, are ugly, don't you think?"

Aunt Cal rolled her eyes and walked back to the window.

"Just before the curve, I remember considering *Dutch* or *clutch* or *hutch*. 'In the hutch of my heart, I love you so mulch.' "

"How about *touch?* It sounds pretty good," Ariel suggested again.

"That's it!" Lou almost bounced off the couch. "*Touch!*" She eased back against the pillows. "I remember. 'I send you a rose, so soft to the touch, to tell you I love you so very mulch!' "

"Oh, Louisa," Aunt Cal sighed in a voice so soft Trevor couldn't believe it belonged to her.

"Is that the way you write your poems, Miss Lou?" Ariel sounded as if the answer really mattered.

"No one with a brain writes anything when she's driving a car!" Aunt Cal shouted.

"Now, Calla," Lou soothed, "don't you get ideas when you're driving?"

"Not when I'm going around a curve."

Lou chuckled. "I wasn't going *around* a curve. I was going *across* it!"

"Time for rest." Melva bustled in from the hall. "Doctor's orders, and mine, too."

Aunt Cal disappeared into her study. Ariel left on her bike. Trevor started for the sun-room, then stopped and walked back to the library doorway.

"Lou, can I ask you a question?"

"Of course, Trevor. Come in. It's still morning, and I don't need a nap."

He wondered if he should tell her that her face was gray, not tanned the way it usually was. He wanted to come right out and ask about the Bookfinder, but he didn't want her to laugh at him, so he said, "It's about Ariel. She's sort of weird, isn't she?"

Lou thought for a minute. "Weird? No more than the rest of us. Unusual, perhaps. Imaginative, and quite well adjusted, considering . . ."

"Considering what?"

Lou rearranged her pillows. "Considering that her parents abandoned her when she was a baby and that her only family is her grandfather and Melva."

Ariel hadn't been lying, and if she'd been telling the truth about that. . . . "Do you think you can believe everything she says?"

Lou looked startled. "I would think so. Her grandfather is impeccably honest. Perhaps it runs in the family."

Trevor couldn't go on. He couldn't make himself ask the question. "Impeccably honest." Trevor touched his pocket. He hadn't mailed that last letter to the Bookfinder.

Freddie Ackerman, his battles ended, took a deep breath and squared his shoulders. The war was over; all that was left for him was to resign his commission, to accept his fate with dignity and honor.

He pulled the envelope from his pocket and handed it to Lou. "I think this belongs to Aunt Cal. Maybe she can use the stamp on something else."

Lou looked at the address, and then closed her eyes. Trevor waited, but she didn't move. At first he thought she'd dropped off to sleep. Old people did that sometimes. Or maybe she'd had a concussion that the doctor hadn't noticed. He thought about calling Melva, when Lou whispered, "Yes."

"Ariel said"—he tried to choose his words carefully— "that the Bookfinder is really Aunt Cal."

"Yes?" she said again. She seemed to mean "go on." He went on.

"I wrote to say that the book didn't belong to me."

"We were sure you would." Her eyes were wide open now.

"Why didn't you tell me?" That was the question that bothered him most.

Lou took a deep breath. "When your mother wrote to us, we didn't have the slightest idea what to do. Imagine! A twelve-year-old boy! I thought we should find you a job for the summer, but Calla said we should turn you loose and let you run."

She sat up, putting both feet on the floor and laying the unopened envelope on the coffee table. "You can't believe how happy we were when you accidentally found that book and tried to sell it. I'll admit, it was *my* idea to send you off to find all those places. Like a treasure hunt, I thought. And it was kind of fun for Freddie Ackerman, wasn't it?"

He didn't have a chance to answer because Melva appeared at the door. "You still here, Trevor?"

"We had a little secret to discuss." Lou winked at Trevor.

"Well, here's another little secret. You forgot to take your pills. You were supposed to have one an hour ago."

"Pills!" Lou sputtered. "I quit taking pills long ago, when I couldn't remember what they were for."

"These are to make you relax," Melva ordered. "Oh, and Trevor, there's a letter from your mother out on the hall table."

"It's not Monday," Trevor objected. "Her letters come on Monday."

"Monday or not, it's there on the table," Melva insisted.

Something must have gone wrong already. Maybe Charlie hadn't worked out. That would be too bad, because Charlie had some possibilities. He always tried to act like a father, and if he could just learn not to *act*, he'd be okay. Being a father should be easier than being a great-aunt.

Trevor carried the letter to the back steps, where he'd spent most of the summer. He skipped past the "Dearest." Mom and Charlie were coming home earlier than they'd planned! His throat tightened. Next weekend! He could catch a flight home and spend the rest of the summer with them!

His exile was over and he was free! He could mall-crawl, play Nintendo, and watch all the TV he wanted. He could listen to his own stereo instead of Aunt Cal's steady diet of operas and concertos and symphonies.

He looked at the rest of the letter. "Charlie and I miss you, but if you want Blue Isle for the rest of the summer, we'll understand."

They were giving him a choice! He could go or stay. He liked the way the words made him feel.

Trevor folded the letter carefully and put it back into the envelope. Charlie was working out after all.

That evening, Melva served dinner in the library. Aunt Cal ate from a hand-painted wooden fold-up table, Lou from a tray beside the couch, and Trevor sat on the floor.

"An indoor picnic," Lou said. "How original."

It was nice, and relaxed, especially since no one had said anything about the Bookfinder or Trevor's letter. He hadn't planned on mentioning what his mom had written, but the words popped out. "Mom and Charlie are coming home next weekend."

Aunt Cal put down her fork. Lou stopped chewing.

"*Next* weekend?" Lou's voice was flat.

Aunt Cal stared out the window as if she'd just discovered the cove. It was uncomfortably quiet.

He'd thought they'd be happy to get rid of him, but they weren't smiling. Would they miss him too? He'd never been missed before today—dismissed after his required time with whichever parent, but not missed. He carefully cut a bite of Melva's Swiss steak and looked up from his plate. Neither of his aunts was eating.

"I have a choice." He put his plate on the floor and sat up on his knees. "I can fly home next weekend, or I can stay till summer's over. I could help around here until Lou gets well. I could bike in for the mail and even weed the flower beds, if they need it."

"How nice of you, Trevor, to think of us," Lou said softly.

"Whatever you like, Trevor," Aunt Cal boomed, and smiled down at him.

Trevor picked up his plate. Was this what it felt like to be part of a family?

Summer was over.

Aunt Cal said so the next morning as she thumbed through her appointment book. "Autumn comes early to Blue Isle."

"Probably because you're so far north and surrounded by water," Trevor suggested.

"Not really. Autumn comes when the off-islanders go home."

"Like me?"

Aunt Cal looked up, frowning from forehead to chin. "You're family, Trevor," she snapped. "If we skip your parents, you're a third-generation Blue Islander."

Now, sitting on the front steps and looking across the cove to the bay beyond where the early sun was turning the Camden Hills into a band of gold and green, he thought about the end of summer. Usually he couldn't wait for summers to be over—long, boring ones with Real-Father and Daphne and the *its* and *thems*, or never-ending camp with hikes and blisters and rain and soggy food and cold bedrolls. When life was as boring as skim milk, time stood still; fun times whizzed past.

It would be a whole, long year before there'd be another summer. Aunt Cal had already called and reserved his seat on the plane home, next to the window. Maybe he'd be able to spot Blue Isle from the air. He hadn't bothered to look on the flight in. Melva would drive him to Bangor early the next morning.

Only one day left of a whole summer!

He could understand now why Lou had told him once, "I don't like November—mostly because it turns into December." Endings weren't any fun.

Lou was locked in her cell working on the 110 Valentine cards she had to have ready by September. Aunt Cal was reading in the library. Melva was vacuuming the living room. It could have been any day at Skyfield instead of the last of his summer.

Bike tires whirred and gravel crunched. Trevor turned to see Ariel lean her bicycle against the corner of the house and walk toward him. The sun turned her hair to strawberry blond. How could he ever have thought it looked like straw? And what he'd thought was pudgy now fitted into dazzling white shorts and a soft green shirt that made her eyes seem to glisten.

174

"What are you doing here?" It wasn't what he wanted to say, but he still didn't know *how* to say what he meant.

Ariel looked down at him and grinned. "Let's ride down to Stoneport. I thought we could try again."

"What for?" That wasn't what he wanted to say either.

"For fun and because you're leaving tomorrow." She flipped a strand of golden hair back from her face. Jessica was always doing that, too.

"Why not?" For some reason he was having trouble putting more than two words together. Jessica would have called him "syntax-impaired." She did that a lot—made up names to call people. For the first time, it occurred to him that, all in all, Jessica was not a very nice person.

The ride to the end of the island was full of smells: tangy salt air, the bitter odor of firs mixed with some perfume Ariel was wearing. They stopped halfway down and Trevor bought two cans of cola at a gas station. They sat by the side of the road and drank them, not talking, but he didn't feel uncomfortable with the silence. He hadn't even thought of taking his Walkman.

It was well past noon before they reached the harbor town. The streets were lined with gift shops and tearooms and antique stores and—kids!

"This is my friend Trevor," Ariel said to some guy called Scott, who looked as if he could do ninety push-ups on one breath.

"Yo, Trevor," he said, and didn't even laugh at the name.

Then there was Heather, taller than Ariel and a little

thinner, but not half as pretty. "You'll never guess in a million years what happened last night!"

"What?" gushed Jami, whose hair was so permed it looked as if she'd been electrocuted.

"Homer busted a dealer! Some kid from Green Hill."

"Not Homer?"

"Honest!" squealed Heather. "And Homer got his picture in the *Green Hill Chronicle*. He set up a stakeout somewhere on Blue Isle, but he won't tell where. He says it's only for confidential police files."

Freddie Ackerman, U.S. Army, retired, hid a trium-phant smile. His lips would remain as tightly sealed as Homer's files.

"Homer would be up for a big promotion," Scott said, looking only at Ariel. "He'll never get it, though."

"Why not?" Trevor asked, trying to include himself in the conversation.

"Because he's going to retire and build wooden lawn ducks. The kind whose wings turn in the wind," Scott answered without looking at him.

Ariel ignored Scott and turned to Trevor. "He always said he'd quit when he made one big arrest, and this must have been it."

Trevor didn't know whether to feel sorry or glad to have seen Homer end his career.

The kids drifted away, and Ariel and he parked their bikes and bought hot dogs and some fries and walked down to the dock where Ariel's grandfather kept the mail boat.

176

"Come on," she said as she climbed over the side. "Let's eat on board."

They sat cross-legged on the deck as gulls dipped down overhead, begging for food. The heavy old boat bobbed gently as a light breeze rippled the water into bursts of silver.

"Why didn't we come down here before—and meet all those kids?" Trevor asked.

"You didn't believe me." She dangled a lone french fry in the air.

"That was two weeks ago. I mean way back when I first got here and when I met you."

"I wasn't sure I liked you." She popped the fry into her mouth and stared off across the harbor. "I thought you were permanently plugged into those earphones."

"Did you come down here by yourself?" He was beginning to wish he could start the whole summer all over again.

"Sometimes, when there wasn't anything else I wanted to do and when I wasn't helping Grandpa." She did that thing again with her hair.

"Then how come you asked me to come with you *today*?" He hoped he didn't get a Jessica answer.

She turned and looked directly at him for the first time since they'd boarded the boat. "Because . . . because I think you're special . . . and I *do* like you, Trevor Ackerman."

He couldn't remember when anyone had said they actually liked him. He was pretty sure his mom did, although he couldn't remember her mentioning it. He thought his real dad might, but he never talked about things like that. As for his other fathers and mother, he knew they felt he was just something that came along with an arrangement . . . except maybe Charlie. He couldn't tell about Charlie yet.

He tried to swallow the last bite of hot dog, but it stuck in his throat. Jessica's calling him a *wimpkin* that last day of school started to fade from his mind. "A *wimpkin*," she'd explained, "is smaller and wimpier than a wimp."

Trevor, the special Trevor, reached over, clasped Ariel by the shoulders and, pushing his face so close to hers that he felt the side of her nose against his, said what he'd been afraid to say to her all summer. "And I like you, Ariel, very much."

He kissed her, right on the lips, and felt her lips kiss back. Jessica didn't know what she was talking about! Girls didn't kiss boys. Boys didn't kiss girls. They kissed each other! The last swallow of his hot dog floated gently down his throat.

He wasn't sure whether it was the bobbing of the boat or the flush of warmth that started at his toes and crawled up his back or the taste of Ariel's last french fry on his lips that made him feel as if he had caught a glimpse of a wonderful new life opening up.

THAT NIGHT he packed his bags, dumping the contents of his dresser drawers onto the bed and sorting and folding and stuffing—the whole Blue Isle summer into two suit-cases and a backpack.

Miranda York was stuck at the back of the dresser drawer. He knew he should return it to Aunt Cal, but he'd wait until his aunts were in bed and sneak down to leave it on the library desk. He'd be gone before they noticed it.

He reached into the drawer, felt around and pulled out . . . not *Steps on the Stairs*, but *The Secret of the Island: A New and Exciting Miranda York Mystery*.

The jacket, so shiny and slick it felt like glass, showed a pine-covered island in the background, with a modern Miranda York standing in the prow of a boat—a Miranda that looked exactly like Ariel, if Ariel had been older and thinner. Even the pages smelled new as he flipped through them.

What he saw next made him sit down on the edge of his bed and stare. On the title page, written in actual handwriting by a real person, was: "To Freddie Ackerman —'We are such stuff as dreams are made on.' Flavia LaRue."

Aunt Cal must have bought it for his going-away present when she was in New York. She must have met Flavia LaRue and had her autograph the book for him.

He'd read it on the plane. He laid it down on the dresser and turned back to his suitcases. There was a light tap on the door.

"Trevor?" It was Melva. "Here's the rest of your clean clothes from the dryer."

"Come in, and thanks."

"Almost done packing, I see," she remarked as she put a pair of Levi's and a couple of T-shirts on his dresser. "Oh," she said picking up the new book, "Did Miss Calla give you this?"

"I think so. I found it in my drawer." He didn't try to explain more, but Melva wasn't paying any attention as she leafed through the book.

"We haven't received one at the library yet. This must be an advance copy. Maybe she can relax now that this is published."

"You mean Flavia LaRue?"

"I mean your Aunt Calla. Now things should settle down to normal for a while." She closed the book, rubbed her hand across the cover, and almost reluctantly laid it down.

"You mean Aunt Cal sells those books?"

"Sells them? Well, in a way. Don't you know that she writes them?"

He felt his brain whirl, and flashes of his aunt whizzed past his eyes like lights on a video game. "Honest?"

"Not many people know. It's some kind of secret with her publisher, but I thought you did. She's been Flavia LaRue for the last forty years, and she'll probably start another book this fall, if she hasn't begun one already."

"That's what she does every morning?" He realized he'd been holding his breath.

"Every morning," she repeated, "but I'd better let you finish packing. Remember, we have to leave early for the airport. Better sleep fast."

Sleep? He had a whole summer to relive! He had to fit Flavia LaRue into Aunt Cal. No wonder she was so big. It must have taken a lot of sitting to write books for forty years.

Beethoven's Fifth exploded like a blitz of bombs from the stereo downstairs. Aunt Cal had told him that that was the source of Winston Churchill's "V for Victory" sign during World War II.

He pulled open his bedroom door and marched through the hall and down the stairs. He planned his words carefully.

"Thank you for the book," he'd say. "And have you begun the next one?" And Aunt Cal would say, "Freddie Ackerman, you knew about it all along, didn't you?" He'd smile, his eyes nothing but slits, and say, "Of course I did, Flavia."

Aunt Cal was in her usual chair, only her feet showing beneath her caftan—a blue-and-green caftan. Lou was across from her in a straight chair, feet tucked under as if she were going to spring into action at any moment.

"Packing done?" Lou turned down the volume on the stereo.

"Almost." He couldn't remember what he'd planned to say.

"I hope Beethoven doesn't disturb you. It does start

off with a bang, doesn't it? But then, he was deaf for a great part of his life."

"It didn't bother me." Trevor stood in the doorway. "About the book," he began.

"We're glad you found it. Calla picked it up in the city, and we thought you might like to have it to remember Blue Isle by."

"That's where it takes place?" He'd been right. The picture looked like the island and Ariel. "Thank you," he managed to say. "I'll read it on the plane. And it's autographed. That might make it very valuable some day, mightn't it?" He looked at Aunt Cal.

"It all depends on how badly someone wants it and how much they are willing to pay."

"Oh, I won't ever sell it." In fact, he wouldn't even show it to Jessica, though he would write and tell Ariel about it.

He knew he didn't need to mention Flavia LaRue. Secrets like that were his family's business.

He *didn't* know how to say good-bye the next morning as he stood on the steps, Melva's car barely visible through the fog.

"Let's get going," Melva called.

Trevor opened the screen door.

"Do write. Your letters are so interesting," Lou said as she held open the door. "Tell us about all of your families."

"Come back next summer, Freddie Ackerman," Aunt Cal whispered as she spread her arms.

The screen door banged behind him as Freddie Ackerman, the *real* and *original* Freddie Ackerman, ran toward Melva's car, Aunt Cal's hug warm against his chest and Lou's tears damp upon his cheek.

He tried to spot Blue Isle from his window seat on the plane, but it was hidden in the fog and the mist.